Hey you!

An alternative novel
for young people

Steve Tash

First published in 1999 by
KEVIN MAYHEW LTD
Buxhall
Stowmarket
Suffolk IP14 3DJ

0 1 2 3 4 5 6 7 8 9

ISBN 1 84003 270 7
Catalogue No 1500235

Edited by David Gatward
Front cover designed by Jonathan Stroulger
Illustrated and designed by Jonathan Stroulger and Steve Tash
Typesetting by Jonathan Stroulger
Printed and bound in Great Britain

contents

contents contents contents contents contents contents contents contents contents

ACKNOWLEDGEMENTS

The publishers wish to express their gratitude to the following for permission to include their copyright material in this publication:

Tony Castle for extracts from his book(s) *Quotes and Anecdotes* by Anthony P. Castle, published by Kevin Mayhew Ltd.

Guinness Publishing, 338 Euston Road, London, NW1 3BD, for the records from *The Guinness Book of Records,* 1998 edn. © 1997 Guinness Publishing Ltd. *The Guinness Book of Records* is the trademark of Guinness Publishing Ltd.

David Higham Associates Ltd, 5-8 Lower John Street, Golden Square, London, W1R 4HA, for the extract from *Charlie and the Chocolate Factory* by Roald Dahl, published by Penguin Books.

Hodder & Stoughton Ltd, 338 Euston Road, London, NW1 3BH, for the extracts from *Know Your Faith* by John Young. Also for the scripture quotations which are taken from *The New International Version* © Copyright 1973, 1978, 1984 by International Bible Society. Used by permission. All rights reserved. 'NIV' is a registered trademark of International Bible Society. UK trademark number 1448790.

Inter-Varsity Press, 38 De Mountfort Street, Leicester, LE1 7GP, for the extract from *Basic Christianity* by John Stott.

Penguin UK, 27 Wrights Lane, London, W8 5TZ, for the extract from *Heard it in the Playground* by Allan Ahberg.

SPCK, Holy Trinity Church, Marylebone Road, London, NW1 4DU, for the extract from *Science and Christian Belief* by John Polkinghorne, 1994.

Special thanks go to Hazel St. John for permission to use Patricia's stories. Further stories by Patricia St. John can be read in *Would you believe it?*, published by HarperCollins and in the USA under the title *Stories to Share*.

Every effort has been made to trace the owners of copyright material and we hope that no copyright has been infringed. Pardon is sought and apology made if the contrary be the case, and a correction will be made in any reprint of this book.

FOREWORD

Pete's growing up and it's confusing . . .
Do big boys cry? How do you cope when one girl is on your mind?
What do you do when death turns up?

Who is speaking where mind and spirit meet? Pete won't always be able to forget. He is waking up and will never be the same again.

If this book were a box of sweets it would be 'Allsorts'.

You can read it, study it, talk about it, discuss it with your friends. It is a short journey in Godtalk.

- Who made me and the world?
- Why is it wonderful and horrible?
- Is Someone doing anything at all about injustice,
  poverty, racism, fear, death?
- Is there something more?
- Who is the God-Man?
- Is he interested in my issues?

This is a story to stretch your imagination.
Will you be the same again?

This book is dedicated to
Beth, Anna and Michael

Reaching out a pale bare arm from under the soft duvet, he neatly prodded the little black square on the CD player. Heavy pounding music was instantly sucked from the bedroom back into the silvery disc. His other hand dropped the *Beano*. The light went out. He slept.

He sat up, muzzy head full of questions. Who said that? What the . . .? Where am I? What's the time? The thought 'time' was interrupted by the electronic beepety-beep of his clock.

Mum called upstairs, 'Pete, Coco Pops or Ready Brek?' He loved Ready Brek but would never have told his friends.

'Ready Brek, ta.' He slipped out of bed, sat on it, scratched his chin. Picking at a thick yellow toenail, he wondered where the night had gone and who had called.

CHAPTER 2

3.05 pm. Thundery clouds outside the classroom. Getting dark early. Pete looked up from the bearded yellowy figure of Moses leading the Jews into Canaan and wished he'd brought his coat. 'It's gonna chuck it down,' he thought.

The class were all quiet, steadily working or dreaming in the fluorescent strip light.

'It's gonna chuck it down in a minute,' he whispered.

'What?' Lee let his fingers, grubby with felt tip, stop their picture of an Egyptian being swamped by the sea. His picture was awful; too much red.

'It's gonna chuck it down,' whispered Pete again, this time nodding his head to the window.

'Yeah.' Lee wasn't at all interested in the weather.

'What's all the red for?' Pete looked at Lee's soiled RE exercise book. Its corners were folded over and the book would never again lie flat on the table.

'It's blood,' whispered Lee defensively.

'No blood when you drown,' smiled Pete.

'How do you know?'

Pete was more interested in the splashes on the window pane and didn't answer.

'Anyway,' said Lee, 'it's the Red Sea, in'it?'

They both giggled and put their heads down to their work. Mr Hanks looked up from the front. The boys checked whether he'd heard them at exactly the moment he'd looked up. Boys' eyes met teacher's.

'You two!'

Their brains cleared.

'What's going on?'

Their tongues froze. Pete had that Ready Brek feeling.

'Get on with your work,' ordered Mr Hanks.

'Get on with your work,' said Paul Bayliss imitating Mr Hanks' voice.

'Paul Bayliss, imitation is another of your many weaknesses,' sighed Mr Hanks, almost yawning. He was old and it was the last lesson.

'Stuff you,' muttered Bayliss.

'I beg your pardon?' Hanks was not yawning now but was slowly rising to his feet, both hands on the desk, ready on the starting-blocks. The geriatric 100-metre sprint.

'Nothing, Sir,' lied Bayliss. But Bayliss hadn't judged the volume of 'Stuff you' well enough. All the class had heard. Hanks knew that they'd all heard. He knew that they knew that he must do something. Bayliss knew too and took the initiative. A storm broke in his head.

Bayliss swore obscenely, accusing Hanks of always picking on him. The classroom, although still before, was now electrostatic. Whatever frustrations Bayliss had with home (if it was) and with the universe in general were chewed between angry teeth and formed into words like dark, thick bubbles of gum. Bayliss, the Moses, leading the cause of oppressed children against the merciless Egyptian schoolteachers.

Pete's palms sweated. He kept his eyes fixed to his textbook. He'd never heard a boy swear four letters at a teacher before, or seven letters and more fours and 'stupid old twit' and more sevens, and Pete seemed to burn inside with 'I don't want to be here'.

Nobody dared catch the eye of teacher, each other or Bayliss. Keeping out of it was so necessary that it drove teeth together and tongues to dryness and heads to shiver. Keep

your head down. Keep your head down, no blanks being fired. This is live.

Silence. Rain arrived to pelt the window, like kids in a playground hurrying to see the fight.

What happens when the world leans sideways? This wasn't real. This isn't how it is.

Pharaoh Hanks coughed. A lifetime as a teacher but still flustered. A little afraid, he spoke softly. Everyone's tight stomachs relaxed just a bit.

Bayliss needed an order. He was as helpless at this second as a non-swimmer drowning, as a baby dumped with no breast.

He had but one word left and could never have said it anyway. Help.

'Leave the room, Bayliss.'

'Yes, Sir.'

Bayliss obeyed and walked with eyes front to the door. He felt relief. Hanks followed and felt the same relief.

Slowly the rest of the class looked up – made wide eyes and open mouths to each other. The classroom breathed again.

The bell went. They packed their bags and left the room unusually quietly and quickly as if further explosives might be hidden in the room, set to detonate at any time.

The megaton weapon of authority fell heavily on Bayliss. He would have to lead other oppressed workers out of a different school in future.

Lee unclipped the padlock holding his and Pete's bikes against a shed upright. The rain attacked the tin roof like

R.D.nstruction
R.K.nowledge
R.S.tudies
R.E.ducation
R.? ????????

God at school?

Heard it in the playground,
telling on you.
Heard it in the playground,
that's not fair.

12

automatic gunfire. It fell in sheets, curtains and blankets just beyond their tin umbrella roof. They waited a few minutes for it to stop.

'My heart was thumping something rotten,' said Pete. 'I dunno why he flipped.' They were enjoying the post-mortem in the fresh early evening air and space. It felt safe after the classroom. They were free to laugh and breathe.

'Serves Hanks right anyway,' said Pete, pronouncing his final judgement as he mounted the saddle and drew up the right pedal. 'Religion is so boring.'

'Boring Snoring,' said Lee.

'He'll have us making bricks without straw next week.'

'You what?'

'Don't matter.'

They rode out into the deluge leaving thin tyre lines in the shining wet road and were drenched in seconds.

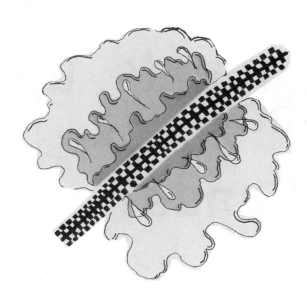

Hands up
Hands up
if you
think
you should
learn
about God
at school?

Hands up
Who
made
hands?

How many pupils receive free schooling in England?

a. 4 million

b. 7 million

c. 10 million

How many schools are there in the state-funded system?

a. 15,000

b. 18,000

c. 22,500

In the state-funded system, the Anglican church has over 5,000 schools, and the Roman Catholic church has over 2,500 schools.

CHAPTER 3

Pete didn't know whether he snored in his sleep, but the words 'Boring Snoring' heaved soft and loud as he drifted away. Boring . . . Snoring; Boring . . . snoring. The words became footholds and handholds as he, step by step, breath by breath climbed a steep rocky cliff. He panted. He needed more strength to continue his climb.

'Hey you!' That voice again.

The concentration of climbing was more important than answering.

'Hey you! Why don't you answer?'

Pete stopped on good holds and managed a breathless, 'Who are you?'

'Never mind now.'

Pete could see no one but the wind was strong and he had to hold on.

'He made all this,' said the voice. 'Look below. The sea, the birds, the air, the space . . . be careful . . . He made all this.'

'Who did?' Pete answered but wanted to keep moving. His limbs were aching. A slight shaking came into his left leg. He was 1000 feet up a sheer face with only air between his feet and the waves far below. Pete looked down, his stomach turned, he gasped. He grabbed the rock tighter. His head felt dizzy. Gulls circled and cried hundreds of feet below.

'Isn't he clever?' said the voice.

'Who?' Pete was getting panicky.

'God of course.'

The words 'Boring Snoring' floated past pulled by a light aeroplane.

'God made the world, it was beautiful, it was for you to

enjoy.' The voice was everywhere; it was in the air, it was on the wind. 'God wanted you to enjoy him.'

'Why don't we then?' Pete, although his body was shaking with the thought of the drop below, felt clever. Felt like Bayliss outsmarting the voice.

Creator Good Creator C   Creator Good
Creator Good C   reator Good
Creat~   eator Good
And God   •   • ator Good
said • • •   •   ud Creator Good
C   Good
Cr **Let there be** Good saw all that he had made
Creator Good Crea It was very good.
Creator Good Cre good, but very good, very
Creator Good Cre badly something is
Creator Good Cre wrong.
Creator Good Creator

all that is, depends now and always   Good
on the freely exercised will of God.
Clearly we cannot perform the ulti-   Good
mate experiment: remove the divine   Good   Creator Good
presence and see if the universe dis- Good   Creator Good
appears.   Good   Creator Good
                                          Good   Creator Good
J. Polkinghorne.   Good   Creator Good

Pete had strength left for one action. He could speak or move to safety. He took breath to announce his last but victorious words – 'God's not there.' The effort to speak made him lose his hold. He was falling over and under. Down, dowwwn, dowwwwwwn. The rush of the air and the speed amazed him. He braced himself for . . .

18

He woke in his bed, as his body, stiff like iron, seemed to break.

'Sorry, Pete.' Mum's familiar voice made his body relax. He breathed air again and felt the warm giving mattress beneath him – he stopped anticipating an icy shattering of his body.

'No Ready Brek.'

''s OK, Mum . . . Got any beans? I feel really hungry.'

'I'll have a look.' Mum put down her furniture polish tin on the CD unit and went in search of beans. Baked beans on toast was an unusual breakfast for Pete.

He ate hungrily without a word to Mum. She was listening to Radio 2 over a cup of tea and a cigarette. His mind was confused. He knew he'd been dreaming but only remembered falling. A bean stuck to his cheek.

'Are me football boots clean, Mum?'

'Why?'

'Why?' thought Pete. 'Silly question.'

''cause I want to go swimming,' he said sarcastically. Mum drew a long drag on the cigarette, gulped the smoke, then laughed in clouds of it. She looked closely at Pete. She knew something. Pete could tell her cheeky chuckle anywhere.

'Why do you want your football boots?' She baited the hook. Pete sat.

'What's she on about?' he thought. 'Friday – football periods 3 and 4 before lunch, same every Friday since term began.' He just looked up, the bean fell off into the others.

'Didn't you play football yesterday?' she played her catch skilfully.

'Oh . . . yeah!' Pete smiled, embarrassed. 'It's Saturday.'

She landed it – a whopper.

'I'm off back to bed.'

Mum playfully called out as his bare feet ran up the stair carpet. 'Sleep well – see you for lunch.' She'd get all sorts done with him out of the way.

It was dark and warm underwater. Pete looked down on a watery city where naked women looked and laughed at him. He felt humiliated. His own naked adolescent body was too young for them. He felt shy like in the school showers. He swam past hundreds of bodies romping and laughing and screaming. A woman strangled herself. The sea city was full of floating rubbish. Men were punching babies and the water was swearing aloud. Fights, stealings, wars, perversions, filled his vision. An armed robber swam past. Someone fire-bombed a church. Fire burned in the water; the church fell. Others made bombs to kill the planet.

Pete lay on his back coughing and choking and drowning, awaiting the swirling whirlpool which was coming nearer all the time. Pete could see its boiling white bubbles, teeth-like, eating their way through the water towards him.

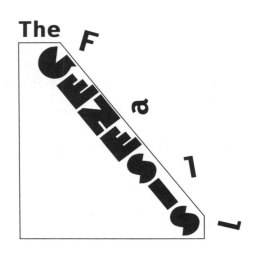

The **F a l l**

Genesis explains the origin of why things went wrong. Read Genesis, chapter 3.

Do you feel the story actually happened like this?

Do you feel this is a kind of early parable to explain why evil exists in the world?

List the consequences of this first disobedience of God.

'For when you eat of it, you will surely die.' (Genesis 2:17)

This is often described as The Fall

Adam and Eve *were so close to God before the disobedience. Now they are driven out.*

The New Testament takes the story very seriously.

Luke 3 traces Jesus' family ancestry back to Adam.

Romans 5 explains how sin and death entered the world through Adam and are passed like infection to everyone.

1 Corinthians 15: 'For as in Adam all die, so in Christ all will be made alive.'

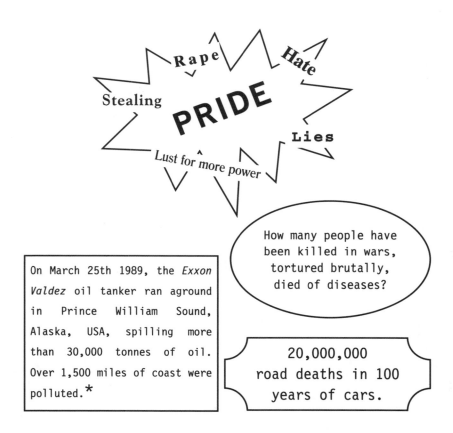

Rape   Hate

Stealing   **PRIDE**

Lies

Lust for more power

How many people have
been killed in wars,
tortured brutally,
died of diseases?

On March 25th 1989, the *Exxon Valdez* oil tanker ran aground in Prince William Sound, Alaska, USA, spilling more than 30,000 tonnes of oil. Over 1,500 miles of coast were polluted.*

20,000,000
road deaths in 100
years of cars.

Estimate . . . tropical forests are being cut down at a rate equivalent to 200 football pitches every minute!!!!!!!!*

CHAPTER 4

Pete looked out of the grimy window of the bus on to crowded streets of Saturday shoppers. The bright sunlight reflecting on the filthy window hurt his eyes and obscured the view. He saw everything through stains and streaks. Mum sat beside him, straight-backed, both hands clutching her shopping bag on her lap.

He'd taken a bath after waking at 11.30 am. Mum had chuckled again when he'd said 'bath' and made old jokes about birthdays and girlfriends. He hadn't remembered the dream but just felt grubby after it, on the inside, as if the beans had been filled with soot and dust and had burst out into his system.

The bus stopped. He looked out. Groups of lads were swigging from tins. Some had bare chests in the sun. Several girls in black tee shirts hung around them. Two market stalls sat in piles of rotten vegetable leaves and vendors shouted things as they mopped their brows. A young mum was bending down to sort out a sticky lolly and a screaming toddler. Sale and bargain posters plastered the shop fronts.

Pete wasn't a great thinker but the word 'messy' did cross his bored brain as he took in what he saw. The bus began with a jolt and the whining engine took them another step nearer Nan's.

Nan's was all right. Her milkshakes tasted somehow older than Mum's but he could watch the BBC 2 film or sport at the press of the remote control. Mum's and Nan's chat didn't disturb him. After 'Hi Nan' and a few agreeable 'Yes's' and 'No's' about school he could opt out of the rest. They would just

25

'catch up on the news'. It was a recording Pete knew so he didn't have to listen. There was usually a present though.

S'funny how easy it is to fool grown-ups. Pete was thinking hot angry thoughts. What a stupid present. What a damn silly present. You stupid old woman. Why can't you buy better presents? He would have allowed swearing and abuse to cross his mind but felt a little afraid that Nan and Mum might be mind-readers. They might see his thoughts in a Beano-type bubble above his head. Who knows? He thought, perhaps they know all my thoughts and pretend they don't. It's all one big experiment, I'm the centre of one big universal science lesson. I'm alone. A human guinea pig.

Pete pushed number one. A steaming horse was being covered with a blanket. White numbers and words in boxes were superimposed over the colour picture. A voice, monotonous and gravelly, gave the starting prices. He'd smiled when Nan gave him the present. He'd said kind, thanks-ever-so-much words when removing the W. H. Smith bag. Nan was happy. She hadn't noticed, or hadn't appeared to, Pete's leaden disappointment. A book was bad enough but a thickset paperback with a schoolish textbook front cover and a title, *The Edge of Scientific Knowledge*. What a joke. What a let-down. You joker, Nan. I'm never gonna read this, you know. The only book Pete ever read at home was the elephant joke book.

'How do you know there's an elephant in the fridge?'

'There's a mini parked outside.'

Clever, that one – worth keeping for people who read science stuff.

He pushed number two. The muddy wet winners' enclosure at Goodwood was transformed into golden sand and

sunny white surf. Sailors were dancing and singing with beery beefy voices.

Pete's eyes wandered over the edge of the scientific knowledge, his fingers let the pages flick over. He read snippets . . .

'One particle, such as an electron, can pass through two slits in a sheet of metal at the same time, and meet up again the other side.' Hmm.

He flicked.

'Nobody understands how gravity works.' Is that right?

He flicked.

'If one of a pair of twins goes on a very long journey in space, and then returns to his brother at home, he will now be younger than the stay-at-home brother.' Interesting . . .

Nan's OK, he thought. He was too much into the book to see Nan and Mum look his way and then back to each other, eyebrows raised.

'The only way to explain why the universe is the way it is, apart from believing in a Creator, is to suppose the existence of an infinity of other universes, all totally beyond the possibility of ever being observed.'

'Ever spread chocolate on hot toast and butter?'

It was the voice in the dream again.

Having returned from Nan's after the football results, Pete had let the evening slip by agreeably. The bus ride had taken him from Nan's armchair to his armchair. The afternoon of sitting down had left him tired and it merged into an evening of sitting down. He'd stayed awake for the football but then gone to bed. Several pages of *The Edge of Scientific Knowledge* later he was asleep.

'Delicious, isn't it?' the voice went on. It looked like a man speaking. Pete could only see the back of him. As the man talked Pete knew he had to follow him. He wasn't telling Pete to follow but there was an unspoken involuntary instinct to stay close behind this man.

They walked about four metres apart along a firm, sandy beach. The sea was evening-still and blue. Small waves, little more than ripples, nibbled the beach unhungrily. They had eaten a full meal and were tasting the after-dinner mints just because they were there.

'Come,' the man said but with no words. 'Follow me,' he said without saying. Pete didn't consider not following. He was drawn.

'So the universe is pretty amazing eh?'

'Yes,' said Pete. 'Nan bought me this book from Smith's.'

Pete thought he had something interesting to say to the man, something to offer to the conversation. He was eagerly about to recount some amazing facts about clocks running faster on Jupiter, but the man butted in.

'So you liked it then?'

The question showed foreknowledge of the gift. It was the question of the giver of a gift unfortunately absent at its unwrapping. The questioner also knew of Pete's initial disappointment.

Pete looked up from his sandy toes to the man whose back was still towards him but whose identity became more interesting and mysterious by the minute. Pete noticed the figure's silken golden cape, brilliantly light.

'Who are you? Where are we going?' Pete called.

It was evening and the blazing orange sun was resting

tightrope on the sharp horizon. One tilt of the horizontal line and like a ball the sun would roll down. Yet the light. As Pete looked at the man he realised the main light was coming from the voice ahead and not from the sun out at sea. It was becoming brighter. It was beginning to hurt Pete's squinting eyes.

'Clocks, Space, Earth – he made them all. But like the fresh warm smell of toast becomes covered with the brown thickness of chocolate spread, so the fresh, pure, innocent world was slowly covered. Just a drop from a spoon at first. A tiny pin-prick tendril of chocolate onto the bread, but then faster, icicle-thick dark pouring, a gout, a knife-covering.' Pete shaded his eyes.

'Looks delicious, doesn't it? Sweetly layered, molten, cold. Sink in, teeth, teeth, gums, chew. Yes, it's tasty, but try swimming in it. You did when you fell, and the whirlpool comes ever closer.' The light vanished. Pete sat looking out to sea. It was chocolate-dark. The sun had gone. He made sure his feet weren't sucked by the water's edge.

Has God

got
in
touch
with
us?

Visions
Dreams
Words
Visits
Coincidence

Hebrews 1:1-2

**Many people have
such experiences . . .
. . . what's yours?**

Read the story, read the story ... A fourth mysterious person saves the life of three missionaries. 'Who was that man who sat with you all the night in the moonlight?'

The Guard They Dared Not Kill
By Patricia St John

His name was Upton Westcott and he went out to Zaire as a young man, nearly a hundred years ago, to preach the Gospel to people who in those days were savages and cannibals. Later on, his wife died of black-water fever and Upton became blind. But still he stayed on, directing and organising what by then had become a large and flourishing Mission. He died among the people he loved.

It was on one of his rare visits to England that he told this story. He was an old, white-haired man, but he walked so erect and fearlessly that it was hard to tell that he was blind. His eyes seemed to be looking back to those years long ago, when he was just a young man.

He and his friends had pitched their tent near a cluster of huts not far from the lake. It was a beautiful stretch of water but infested with hippos and crocodiles and behind their tent was the mysterious green border of the jungle. But the people were friendly and brought them bananas and other fruit, and when they had finished their hoeing and fishing of an evening, the villagers would come and squat round the fire and listen to what the young men had to tell them. Gradually a few came to realise that this message of love and eternal life was for them too, and one by one they cast off their

heathen practices, and learned to live as Christians should – honestly, at peace with their neighbours, caring for one another.

They were very brave, those early African converts, for their lives had been haunted by evil spirits and it was hard to believe that this new, loving Father could really keep them safe. There was one witch doctor whom they had always specially feared, whose charms and magic were supposed to take effect all over the district. He was reported to be very angry when he heard that his people were turning to the true and living God, and all waited anxiously to see what his revenge would be.

It was supper time and the kraal was busy with its fires and bubbling clay pots, and Upton and his friends were also cooking when they saw the frightened boy beckoning from the margin of the jungle. They went to speak to him and found that he was trembling and his eyes were full of fear. 'I have come to warn you,' he whispered. 'You must escape tonight. My father will help you. He has a canoe ready and you must be down by the creek before the moon rises tonight. He says it is your only chance.'

'But why should we flee? Who is going to harm us?'

'Why, the Great Witch Doctor. Tonight he sends his killers. At the darkest hour they will attack with spears. You cannot escape them.'

The three held a quick consultation. They had a gun for shooting wild beasts but they did not intend to use it for killing men, and besides, what use would it be if the tent was surrounded by spear-throwers? Also, they had taught these young men and women to rely on God's protection, and they, the Christians, could not run away. In any case, they had

nowhere to run to. Upton turned back to the frightened, waiting boy.

'Thank your father,' he said, 'but tell him that our God has not told us to flee. We will trust in his protection and wait for what comes.'

The boy sped off and the three made ready for bed. They ate their supper as usual and the tropical night came swiftly. Never had they been so conscious of the rustle of leaves, snakes and birds or the soft distant chatter of monkeys. They sat for a time in the door of their tent, praying and waiting.

The moon rose, the world was flooded with silver light, but the three had no desire to go and lie down in the tent. Better, they thought, to meet death in the open, seeing their enemies, than to be cornered like rats in a trap. They had decided not to use the gun. What was the use of killing one or two in front, when six more would be throwing spears from the back? And perhaps they remembered Stephen. He did not die with a gun. He looked up to Jesus.

All night they waited under the fierce tropical stars. Then the moon set. It was the cold eerie hour when mists rise from the lake and the world is shrouded. Perhaps now?

But no one came, and at last the sun rose and the tired young men, who had never expected to see another dawn on earth, watched the mists scatter with new eyes.

Then came the sound of voices at the well, the crackling of fuel and the thud of the hoes, and wreaths of smoke rose from the kraal. Never had life seemed so beautiful! They crawled into their tents and slept soundly, and the little group of Christians creeping up and peeping fearfuly through the flaps, praised God and wondered, for had they not heard

the news and mourned as those who had lost a father? Surely, the hand of the Lord sheltered these teachers.

Months passed, and because no harm came to those who no longer worshipped the spirits, others took heart. Love and freedom were far better than the old bondage of fear. Besides, they were less afraid than they had been, for the old witch doctor seemed to have lost his power. Some said that he was too old and others said that the spirits had forsaken him. Whatever the reason, men feared him no more.

But all the same, Upton was very surprised one day to find the old man kneeling in the doorway of his tent, his finery drooping, his monkey tails flapping. When at last he bowed himself in, Upton saw that he looked weak and hollow-eyed. 'I want to learn about the living God,' he said simply.

They talked for a long time. Upton spoke to him of sin and repentance and he seemed uneasy. There was so much sin; and there was one sin that weighed heavier on his conscience than any other.

'Then confess it that it may be forgiven,' said Upton.

So he told all. It was the night of the new moon, he said, and he had sent his men through the jungle with spears and orders to kill the three, but they came back with their spears clean. They had shed no blood.

'But why?' asked Upton. 'We were unarmed. No one could have prevented them.'

'Because there were four of you,' said the witch doctor. 'My men had no order to kill four, and they could not see who was who. They waited till the mists rose but he did not go away. My friend, who was that man who sat with you all the night in the moonlight?'

But Upton could not answer that question. Had the Lord

himself sat with them or had he sent his angel? He did not know. It was enough for him that they had seen the morning and that the old witch doctor himself was turning to the light of the Lord Jesus.

Psalm 34:7

King David was a poet too. Perhaps he wrote this remembering a brilliant life-saving slingshot.

AngelsAngelsAngelsAngelsAngelsAngelsAngelsAngelsAngel
sAngelsAngelsAngelsAngelsAngelsAngelsAngelsAngelsAnge
lsAngelsAngelsAngelsAngelsAngelsAngelsAngelsAngelsAng
elsAngelsAngelsAngelsAngelsAngelsAngelsAngelsAngelsAn
gelsAngelsAngelsAngelsAngelsAngelsAngelsAngelsAngelsA
ngelsAngelsAngelsAngelsAngelsAngelsAngelsAngelsAngels

The first words of angels when they appear to humans are often, 'Don't be afraid'. Why?

As he came near the place where I was standing I was terrified and fell prostrate. (Daniel 8:17)

When Zechariah saw him, he was startled and was gripped with fear.

'I am Gabriel. I stand in the presence of God and I have been sent to speak to you.'

Do not be afraid, Mary.

Shepherds near Bethlehem see an angel of the Lord . . .

'. . . and they were terrified.'

Swing low, sweet chariot,
coming for to carry me home;
I looked over Jordan,
and what did I see?
A band of angels coming after me.
Coming for to carry me home.

Spiritual, *c* 1850

Angel Action

chains . . . no problem

soldiers . . . no problem

iron gate . . . no problem

READ ACTS CHAPTER 12

גבריאל GABRIEL

מיכאל MICHAEL

Lady put advert in paper to collect stories of angels. Did she get any replies? Hundreds! – from ordinary people who claimed that the experience had only happened once in their lives. This made them sound very true rather than imagination or hallucination.

There was a war in Heaven. Michael and his angels fought against the dragon, and the dragon and his angels fought back.
(Revelation 12:7)

Suddenly a great company of the heavenly host appeared with the angel praising God and saying, 'Glory to God in the highest, and on earth peace to men on whom his favour rests.' Suddenly a great company of the heavenly host appeared with the angel praising God and saying, 'Glory to God in the highest, and on earth peace to men on whom his favour rests.' Suddenly a great company of the heavenly host appeared with the angel praising God and saying, 'Glory to God in the highest, and on earth peace to men on whom his favour rests.' Suddenly a great company of the heavenly host appeared with the angel praising God and saying, 'Glory to God in the highest, and on earth peace to men on whom his favour rests.' Suddenly a great company of the heavenly host appeared with the angel praising God and saying, 'Glory to God in the highest, and on earth peace to men on whom his favour rests.' Suddenly a great company of the heavenly host appeared with the angel praising God and saying, 'Glory to God in the highest, and on earth peace to men on whom his favour rests.' Suddenly a great company of the heavenly host appeared with the angel praising

'Do not forget to entertain strangers for by so doing, some people have entertained angels without knowing it.' (Hebrews 13:2)

Have
angels got
wings? Do they
play harps? Do they
have shiny cherub faces?
Do they look like little children
dressed up for the Christmas play?

God and saying, 'Glory to God in the highest, and on earth peace to men on whom his favour rests.' Suddenly a great company of the heavenly host appeared with the angel praising God and saying, 'Glory to God in the highest, and on earth peace to men on whom his favour rests.' Suddenly a great company of the heavenly host appeared with the angel praising God and saying, 'Glory to God in the highest, and on earth peace to men on whom his favour rests.' Suddenly a great company of the heavenly host appeared with the angel praising God and saying, 'Glory to God in the highest, and on earth peace to men on whom his favour rests.'

More Visions

More Dreams

More Angels

The Bus That Would Not Stop...

by Patricia St John

'Wake up, Fatima, we must be starting; the sun is already over the crest of the hill!'

Fatima yawned and sat up. She and Mary had been sleeping in the village where they went every Tuesday evening to give out medicine and to tell the Gospel message to any who wanted to hear. Menana, a woman whom Mary had first met in her dispensary, had begged them to come and had gladly welcomed them

into her little home. So each week at sunset the thatched hut filled up with a crowd of dark-eyed villagers on their way home from the fields. Some just wanted medicine, but some would stay, crouched round the charcoal, and ask for Bible stories. Sometimes they would discuss a question far into the night and it was often after midnight when they lay down to sleep on the mattresses around the walls. They had to be up early too and get back as fast as they could, for children arrived at about nine o'clock for lessons and their home was about eight miles away. Sometimes they walked the distance, but occasionally they caught a rather irregular market bus that would take them about three miles on their way, as far as a fork in the road.

That early summer morning they started off as usual. The harvest had been reaped and the fields were pale gold stubble, and the dawn wind stirred the threshing floors. Down by the river the Indian corn grew in emerald patches and the figs were ripe for picking. The sky was already bright through the early mists and it was going to be very hot. The sooner they got home the better. And to their great relief, the bus was in sight as they reached the main road – a bus laden with villagers. They managed to squeeze in.

Soon Fatima nudged her, for they were getting near the fork in the road, They rose and battled their way to the front.

'Stop, please,' said Fatima. 'We want to get off here.'

But the driver turned out to be a very surly, unpleasant man.

'No,' he replied, 'I am not going to stop here. This is no proper stopping place. I'm going on to the next bridge. There is another fork there and you can walk back to your village.'

'But,' cried Mary, 'that will take us miles out of our way

down the valley. It will take us hours to walk back up that steep mountainside. Oh, please stop!' And in her heart she cried to God, 'Oh, Lord, we need to get home, and it is getting so hot. Please make him stop.'

But the driver would not be persuaded and there was nothing to do but to go and sit down again. Mary felt very cross indeed but Fatima was surprisingly calm. 'We prayed this morning that all would be well,' she said. 'We shall get back some time. Let us be patient.'

But Mary did not feel at all patient when at last the bus stopped and put them down at the foot of a steep hill, seven miles from home.

They stood gazing down the valley, in case another vehicle was coming but there was nothing in sight. Already the heat was shimmering on the hills, and the river, almost dried up now, trickled between the oleander bushes. They never heard the woman approaching. She had walked down the hill behind them, where they stood, and in her arms was a bundle covered with a cloth. She glanced at Mary, but went straight to Fatima.

'Is that the English nurse?' she demanded.

'Yes, my sister,' replied Fatima.

'Then present me to her,' said the woman.

She was a strong, dark-eyed country woman in a shady straw hat, and a striped cloth round her waist. On her legs she wore leather gaiters to protect her from thorns and snake bites, and round her neck she wore charms to protect her from evil spirits. She came straight over to where Mary stood and drew the cloth away from the bundle in her arms. It was a baby and she had covered its face to keep the flies away from its infected eyes. The lids were swollen as large as

purple grapes and stuck together. What the eyes were like underneath had yet to be discovered.

'I have brought her to you,' said the woman simply.

'How long has she been like that?' asked Mary.

'Four days. She lies crying with her face to the wall and will not suck.'

'But how did you know to come here? It is not market day. There are no others from your village on the road.'

'Last night I knew my child was getting worse. She was burning with fever. I slept with a heavy heart, and as I slept I dreamed. A man came to me dressed all in white and he said to me, "Take that child to the English nurse."

'I said in my dream, "I do not know where she lives nor do I know her."

'And the man in white answered, "Rise at dawn and go down to the main road by the bridge, and there you will find her waiting for you. She will tell you what to do." So I came and you are here.'

So they all set off up the long hill that led home and another bus soon came and picked them up. The woman stayed all day, and by evening, after penicillin injections and frequent irrigations the baby looked much better. Mary sent the mother away with medicine and promised to visit her on the Saturday.

The child recovered completely and that Saturday visit was only the first of many opportunities to speak to that family and village about the love of the Lord Jesus. The mother and her neighbour showed special interest, and Mary and Fatima sitting on the floor, telling them about the Saviour's love, thanked God many times over that he had said, 'Wait' when Mary had prayed that the bus would stop.

CHAPTER 5

Sunday. Pete woke at 10 am. It was quiet. He put on Saturday's clothes and switched on TV.

A man in a white sort-of-nightie and wearing a really long black scarf-thing was reading from a thick green book in the still echo of a church. His voice was posh, his words were unusual. Pete pushed number two.

A man wearing dark-rimmed glasses was speaking to the screen. A blackboard with numbers, crosses and minuses was behind him. It seemed like dull school-stuff. Pete pushed three.

A group of old ladies and a few men standing in rows behind each other were all singing. The music was church-organ-like. They each had a little red book into which they stared. They nearly all wore glasses and the men were mostly balding. Pete pushed four.

A screen full of blue and white sentences which Pete couldn't be bothered to read.

He left the TV on because it was better than leaving the room silent and walked in his socks to the kitchen.

Mum sat quietly smoking over a magazine. Neither said 'Hi', or 'Good morning', or 'Wotcha'. Pete opened the fridge. He listened to its hum. Every sound seemed clearer in the stillness of Sunday morning. Sundays are dead boring, he thought. The light from the fridge into which he poked his head caused his mind to recall a dream. It only lasted a moment.

'Mum, can I have a cheese?' The dream went, smudged out by the thought of a creamy triangle of foil-wrapped cheese.

'Sure.' Mum sat up and stretched. She yawned and spoke

at the same time so that the words became glued together in her throat.

'What are you doing today, Pete?' She breathed out long and deep.

'Parachuting,' he replied quickly. He stuffed the whole triangle into his mouth and left the torn foil on the table beside Mum's magazine.

'See yer la'er.' His own words failed as the creamy cheese stuck to the roof of his mouth.

Most of their communication was jammed by mouthfuls, yawnfuls, generation-gapfuls, TV-fuls, can't-be-botheredfuls.

Pete slipped on his training-shoes and walked out of the back door.

The word parachuting had at least made Mum pull her eyes away from the mag and watch Pete leave.

'Shut the door,' she yelled, but another jamming device was ignorefuls.

Lid lived diagonally opposite across a piece of council green with flower borders. Her name was Lydia but everyone, even some teachers, shortened it. The letters L - I - D were those framed in Pete's mind when he thought of her. And think of her he did. Quite a lot recently. Lee reckoned Pete 'fancied' her. Pete first heard the word on children's TV but Lee was the first real person Pete heard use it.

'Do you fancy her?' Lee had asked after an assembly where Pete had had to sit beside her.

The word first made Pete think of children's parties and frills on iced cakes, but these ideas were swept away, now buried for ever, by the landslide of new ideas: sex, girls, blushing. He practised saying, 'Do you fancy her?' into mirrors.

He'd replied with spitting speed to Lee: 'Naw, you must be joking; she's soppy, a real goody-goody, teacher's pet, legs too long, straggly long hair, thin lips, works hard, not my type, son.' Which all meant . . . yes.

'Are you honestly going parachuting?'

'Yes, next Saturday.'

'How, I mean who with? Where? How did you?'

They were sitting on the kerbstones beside the empty Sunday street. It was warm and the paving slabs were beginning to absorb the heat like stone sponges.

'Weren't you listening during English?'

'Yeah, a bit.'

Lydia had spoken at the front of the class about the parachuting club all her family attend. During that talk Pete had watched her but hadn't really listened to the details.

'Can girls parachute then?'

'Of course . . . you chauvinist.'

Pete smiled without really understanding. Lid was from a family that had a regular dad and brothers and sisters. She was usually well dressed and probably got more pocket money.

'How much pocket money do you get?'

'None of your business.'

'Aren't you scared of dying?'

'Oh don't be morbid.' She did use these unusual words a lot. She offered him a marble-sized mint from a white paper bag.

'Ta.' It felt good being with her. He felt warm, friendly. He felt like he wanted to be kind to her.

They juggled their mints around their mouths with their teeth and didn't speak for a while.

'Define "I fancy her".'
'Well, she turns me on.'
'What, like TV?'
'No, you pillock. You know, 'ormones.'
'What, "fancy" means "hormones"?'
'No . . . I feel for 'er.'
'What, like blindfolded?'
'No! 'spose I sort of love 'er.'
'You gonna marry her then?'
'You fick or somit?'

Possible meanings of 'I fancy her'. Choose your meaning:

1   *She is good looking.*
2   *I want sex with her.*
3   *I am falling in love with her.*
4   *I want to marry her.*
5   *I want to sound cool.*

And I
will
friend
you, if
I may,
in the
dark and
cloudy
day.

(Housman)

48

'I'd better go in now,' Lid said after several minutes, 'we're going out somewhere for the day with a picnic.' She stood up and brushed gravel from her jeans.

Pete needed words to make her stay longer but none would come. He drew something up from his scientific knowledge book. Perhaps people who sat in the clever parts of the classrooms talked about these things.

'Do you know that nobody really knows what we mean by a measurement?'

She paused and looked at him quizzically, sympathetically. 'I'll ask Dad, he teaches physics.' She moved swiftly back into her house but waved a playful 'bye', which lifted Pete's spirits.

Several thoughts swept across Pete's mind as he wandered to his back door. What must a Dad be like? It was a bit scary. How can a teacher be her Dad? Should I work harder at physics? Will she come to the youth club disco with me?

Two things happened that evening which made Pete feel he had swallowed sparklers.

Lid phoned. Her Dad had invited Pete to the parachute club. Pete felt his legs wobble and . . . 'without a parachute from 30,000 feet' kept singing into his thoughts.

Pete had phoned Lee.

'Do you reckon she'll come to the disco if I ask her?'

'Wouldn't be surprised,' replied Lee. 'I heard Jayne Small telling Karen Alsop that Lid fancied you.'

Pete couldn't wait for Monday morning but he couldn't sleep either. His young mind performed somersaults of anticipation. How do you ask a girl out? How do you step out of an aeroplane into very thin air? He didn't know which one terrified him most.

When
did
love
and
sex
get

divor ced

I love you

Does 'I love you' mean . . .
I love me and want you?

What is love for? Does it have a purpose?
What is sex for? Does it have a purpose?

Choose your favourite meaning of 'I love you'.

1. I desire you.
2. I feel a special feeling when we are together.
3. I will always do kind are caring things for you.
4. I promise to share my everything with you.
5. I want to own you.
6. I like being seen with you.

Why did you throw out the other meanings?

Hot sunny day on the ground. Cooler and breezier one thousand feet high up in a basket suspended beneath a barrage balloon. The basket had a tiny gate in one corner, which could be swung inwards to let someone jump out.

First ever jump. Who had checked the parachute? Pete had to trust. He didn't even know how to fold one. Perhaps his 'chute hadn't been checked. There were five of them standing in the basket surrounded and preoccupied with high, silent air.

'Sir?' Pete raised half a voice to ask the soldier-looking man by the little gate a question.

'Please, Sir, did you check my parachute?'

'Be quiet, number two!' The soldier yelled his order.

Blood drained from Pete's face. His stomach was a knot. He felt hollow; his vital organs seemed spooned out by the liver-eating height. Ground, thought Pete; the word sounded so solid and safe and permanent. Will I ever feel it beneath my feet again?

'Ready, number one!' The soldier ordered with a crack-fire shout. He clicked a catch which held the gate closed. It swung open. It was now as easy to step out into the blue space as to jump from the pavement to the road.

'I can't do it, Sir,' said number one.

'Now come on, number one. Hold yourself together.' The soldier hadn't won the sympathetic man-of-the-year award, ever.

'This is what you have trained for, number one; just throw yourself out and away from the basket, your 'chute strap is anchored.'

The soldier waited for ten long seconds for number one, then caught Pete's eye.

'NO,' thought Pete. 'Why did I look up and meet the

soldier's eye?' He knew what was coming. His knees buckled. His thighs felt thinner than jelly, his stomach was liquid like chicken soup.

'OK, number two will show us how to do it – won't you number two?'

Pete opened his mouth to refuse. Only a squeaky whimper came out. He turned to Lid. She smiled, lovingly, and urged him forward. Her confidence that Pete could make the jump made him take the two forward steps to the gate where the only thing beyond was sky. A bird soared, so far below his toes. He swayed. The tiny airfield, thin roads and wide green counties all around swayed. Dizziness, airyness, pukiness!

Pete squeezed his eyes shut.

'He felt like this, Pete.' The voice.

'Who did?' He spoke the words but the soldier beside him didn't hear.

He turned to look at Lid. He loved her. She mouthed the words, 'I love you'. The love gave Pete the strength. He might be able to jump.

'Just like this,' the voice went on. 'He sweated blood, Pete, but love gave him strength. It wasn't a parachute jump. It was a sharp metal point just jabbing his wrist about to be thrust into the flesh and bone, by hammer blows. He held his breath and squeezed tight his eyes. He didn't know if he could go through with it either. He was born for it. Knew he would be crucified. What a digusting word, Pete. Cru . . . ci . . . fied. Intense pain, searing pain, agony. It is everything we are afraid of. Your toes are about to dribble over the edge, but you've got a parachute, he knew he was going to die.'

'He was very brave then,' an afterthought struck Pete, 'or very much in love, or both.'

'Yes, he was very much in love; he still is. And yes, ever so brave. There is a garden you must visit called Gethsemane.' The voice went away. A cool fear took its place and covered Pete like freezing slime.

'GO,' ordered the soldier. Pete had no energy to leap outwards. He simply stepped forward and plummeted down, fast, very fast.

The airfield was approaching quickly. The balloon above seemed to be blasting upwards. He felt overwhelmed by the acceleration. Death would be instant – a ten-billion-ton bang on the head. The airstrip was spinning rapidly, blurring; it looked like the white foaming whirlpool.

Bible stories of God getting in touch with . . .

Moses . . . Exodus 3:4.

Little Samuel . . . 1 Samuel 3:4.

PAUL . . . Acts 9:4.

Us . . . John 1:14.

The Word became flesh
and made
his dwelling
among us.
We have seen
his glory.

Has any visit made a greater impact?

OOOOOOOOFFFFF, a gigantic yank from his harness. Pete was winded. He was floating. The parachute was wide open above his head, broad and safe. The relief he felt was like life pouring into dead bones.

'From Heaven to Earth. Well done.' Someone was floating down beside Pete.

'Don't tangle the chutes,' Pete yelled, anxiously.

'I'm not in a parachute,' someone said. The someone carried on, 'Scary business coming from Heaven to Earth. He showed himself to one tribe first – Israel. He said he loved them and wanted them to be his own. They would show everyone else that he was there.'

'Who was?' Pete asked.

'God.' Pete listened to the messenger with interest. His recent brush with death made him want to hear. 'Then when the time was right, he was born in Israel, a Jew.'

'Why did he have to come down?'

'Too much chocolate spread, Pete. He had to become one of them, to swim around with them, to show them and the whole world that he loved them and would clean them up. Heaven came to Earth, God came to Man. He was God and he was Man so that God and Man would become friends. The Jews and the whole world had got used to living as though God wasn't there and they were heading for the whirlpool, they were falling without parachutes.' Pete shuddered. 'So he came to rescue them.

Pete said, 'I've heard about Mary and Joseph and stables and Bethlehem. Got pregnant didn't she . . . on her own. Bit far fetched, isn't it?'

'Not on her own. By the power of the Most High. That's miraculous. That's beautiful.'

Was Jesus God in person?

A lot of people, like millions and millions
over the last 2000 years, thought so.
Millions still think so.

There are two original paintings by Holman Hunt
of Jesus knocking on the door, called *The Light
of the World*. They hang in St. Paul's Cathedral,
London, and in Keble College, Oxford.

'Here I am! I stand at the door and knock.
If anyone hears my voice and opens the door,
I will come in and eat with him, and he
with me.' (Revelation 3:20)

Now that Pete felt safer as he drifted downwards some of his doubt returned. He asked, 'So who was this guy then, this heavenly freefaller, this Jew, this God-Man, this chocolate spread remover?'

'The one whose hands were spiked to a cross.'

Pete shuddered again.

'Jesus,' the messenger said. 'His name was Jesus.'

Pete looked sidewards to where the voice had come from, but now there was bare blue sky. He heard the canvas creaks of his harness, saw the ground approaching. Someone shouted, 'Feet and knees together, elbows in, knees bent.' It was a hard but welcome touchdown.

Pete washed and dressed quickly. He strode boldly towards Monday morning. He had to be brave. He would ask Lid out. Yes. Definitely. But for a reason he couldn't understand he felt no courage for a trip to her parachute club.

CHAPTER 6

'Come on, Lee, give,' Pete begged.

'All in good time, sunshine. All in good time.'

'You slug, Dixon, you don't know anything.'

The boys walked from the cycle shed to the blue door entrance to year ten's area.

It was a double door. One window was badly smashed and boarded up, the other door hung loose, banging shut loudly behind each child entering. The sprung slow-close mechanism had broken two terms ago. There was an overturned litter-bin beside the door and crisp-papers with banana skins spilled onto the playground. As they passed the rubbish they smelled over-ripe fruit.

'Come on, Lee. Look, if you don't tell me I'll kick your ass,' Pete adopted an American-cop accent.

'Just wait 'til you find out,' Lee taunted.

Both boys actually knew deep down that Lee hadn't phoned Lydia after phoning Pete. Lee, in creating the story and vigorously defending its truth, had begun to believe it. Pete believed it in flashes of doubt. But the game of I-know-something-you-don't had kept them entertained for all the ride to school. Perhaps Lee had invented it because he felt left out of Pete's fast-developing love life. The two boys had been friends since junior school days and although much of their life had included play with girls, they had never dreamed that one would squeeze between their friendship as oil displaces water.

'You don't even know her phone number,' Pete served.

'Looked it up,' Lee backhand.

'What is it then?' Pete forehand.

'Don't you know, Casanova?' Lee forehand smash . . . point.
'I'll ask her then,' Pete served.

'Sure you've got the bottle?' Lee smashed return . . . point. Lee asked the question too sharply, revealing his jealousy. They walked into their form room with a sad and sour taste to their friendship.

Lydia arrived several minutes later, but not alone. Pete watched as she chatted into the room and was soon part of the girls' front corner. He watched her nose and eyes. I do fancy you, he thought, how shall I ask you out?

Form Tutor. Good bloke. 'Open those windows.' Register. Assorted flavours of 'Yes Sirs'. Last week's absent notes. Exit Form Tutor. Bell. Mumble jumble to assembly mumble jumble. 'Quiet, please . . . mumble . . . WILL YOU BE QUIET!' silence . . . sweet paper crackles . . . all look round . . . titter chuckle laugh . . . 'Put it away!' . . . silence . . . Deputy Head . . . results . . . notices . . . short moral story . . . very uninteresting . . . Pete yawns quietly . . . Lee nudges Pete . . . 'Front row, lead out.' Mumble mumble jumble . . . chairs slide and rattle.

Assembly over. Pete brushes Lydia's arm as the mob returns to their form room. He feels good.

English. The oldest member of staff is reading aloud from a novel. The class is following the words from copies of the same novel in front of them. Most are sharing one book between two. Pete and Lee are sharing with Simon, a bespectacled boy with a bad cold. He is, without knowing it, blowing a thin bubble from his nose. It disappears when he breathes in and blows up to pea size when he breathes out. Lee has noticed and feels sick. He half wants Pete to notice too, the other half doesn't want Pete to notice because if each knows

60

that the other knows, the lesson will be spent in the agony of trying not to laugh.

'Sir?' a hand goes up. 'What does justice mean?'

The teacher pauses and thinks. A dozen pairs of eyes look towards the teacher for an answer. No other part of anyone's body moves.

'Anyone?' the teacher's invitation for someone to provide the meaning. Pete and Lee are startled by Simon's voice breaking the silence.

'Something,' sniff, 'that's,' sniff, 'fair, Sir?'

'What do you mean by fair . . . what's fair . . . bumper cars . . . big wheel sort of fair? Better not answer, Simon, we don't all want pneumonia.'

Reid's humour was never hurtful. His kind smiles turned live bullets into blanks. He made the same noises as other teachers but never damaged anyone.

Pete imagined that Lid's dad smiled a lot. His thoughts during the break from reading had already wandered to the front of the class. Meanings of justice weren't being searched out in his mind.

Lee was experiencing disappointment. Simon's words had burst the bubble.

'Well,' continued Mr Reid sitting on the front of the teacher's table, squashing chalk and board rubber.

'Bet he can see Lid good from there,' thought Pete. 'Perhaps I'll become a teacher.'

Mr Reid stood a little and moved the board rubber and piece of chalk. He smacked the dust from his bottom and sat again. Lid and Karen Alsop exchanged a feminine grin behind their hands which propped up their chins.

'Let me tell you something . . . true story from my school

Justice

IF we rip out every verse in the Old Testament concerning justice, oppression and poverty, our Bible will hang in ribbons, e.g.

Proverbs 28:5 . . . Isaiah 10:2 . . .
Isaiah 30:18 . . . Isaiah 61:8
(Jesus probably quoted Isaiah 61
at the beginning of his work: Luke 4:18)
. . . Amos 5:12 . . . etceteraetcetera . . .

Are we still blind?

What does God require?
Isaiah 58:6-14
Micah 6:8

days.' Mr Reid relaxed into an informal posture. It acted like a signal for most of the class to sit back in their chairs and take a deep breath. Lee didn't move since he had positioned himself carefully to watch Simon's nostrils in case of any new stirrings.

'It was quite a strict school . . . all boys . . . we wore uniforms and black jackets. It was the kind of school where boys were often slippered on their backsides with rubber plimsolls . . . sort of trainers.' Most in the class were already wrapped up in Mr Reid's story. It was relevant. It would probably hurt. Some were already smiling.

'That's what schools were like.' Reid's voice was calm, with more nostalgia than malice. He enjoyed telling stories; he thought it was an important part of his teaching skills. This was a good story. He knew it. And it was true.

'A Physics teacher, who smoked about a million cigs a day, would make you bend over and then kick you with his well-aimed Hush Puppy or strike you with a wooden metre rule . . . they called it education.' Mr Reid had already taken side with his audience against the corporal punishment kings of the corridors.

'We had a new Geography teacher called Roberts . . . had a slightly Welsh accent. He'd never really got control of us and one day he just lost it.' What did he mean, everybody in the class thought together. Everybody was lost in Mr Reid's memory. Teacher and whole class were together.

'Just completely lost his cool, went completely O.T.T. He went red, he stamped his foot and yelled with fists clenched and probably toes too, "RIGHT! I'VE HAD IT WITH YOU LOT . . . I'M GOING TO SLIPPER EVERY BOY IN THE CLASS." We all kind of went OOOOOO as if we didn't really believe him. But I

did and the highly charged feeling in the room made my palms sweat.'

Pete thought of Bayliss and wanted to tell Mr Reid about it, but didn't want to interrupt the story.

'We guessed that Roberts wished he hadn't said the words . . . but he had. He'd lose even more respect if he changed his mind. We'd have called him a coward. I can't even remember what we'd done, must have upset him though, he was fuming mad.

'"RIGHT," he said, "WHO'S FIRST?" His challenge was meant to scare us. He could call us cowards and perhaps get out of his threat. He knew he shouldn't have said it and was looking for an escape. If no one volunteered then he was safe. Quite clever really. But not clever enough. From the back of the class Kemp put his hand up. We all looked around, every head turned.

'"Sir," he mumbled in a small voice, "I'll go first."

'"KEMP!" Mr Reid was really into his stride. Kemp! Suddenly transformed into a hero. He was often in trouble with teachers. Seemed to get picked on. I once saw a Maths teacher drag him by his hair around the room. When the teacher let go, a handful of Kemp's hair flopped onto the floor.

'"RIGHT," shouted Roberts, "COME TO THE FRONT. TAKE YOUR JACKET OFF. BEND DOWN." Kemp made his way forward between the single desks and followed instructions. Roberts took a mighty swing with a white plimsoll at Kemp's backside. The sound of rubber hitting tightly stretched trousers was always sickening. THWACKKK.

'Kemp stood up, red-faced. Roberts breathed deeply. "BACK TO YOUR PLACE." Kemp walked the length of the

classroom, crying. We all knew it had gone too far now. It was serious. Would Roberts lamb every boy?

'"RIGHT, THAT'S IT," he seemed almost stuck for words, "KEMP HAS TAKEN THE PUNISHMENT FOR THE WHOLE CLASS." It was a convenient idea of Roberts', who was still looking for a way to escape his own threat. I sat there sweating. I hate confrontations. I thought it OK that Kemp should get it for the rest of us. Roberts began to relax in the silence, he sensed things were going off the boil. But John Barnes had other ideas.

'"Sir," Barnes said calmly, "that's not fair." Roberts' heart sank. "You said you were going to slipper all of us, and Kemp was first, that's all. It's not fair, Sir."

'"RIGHT, BARNES . . . OUT THE FRONT . . . TAKE YOUR JACKET OFF . . . BEND OVER . . ." Another almighty swing, no half-measures, a full man's strength to a boy's backside. THWACKKKK.

'Barnes stood up, red-faced, shaken, and returned to his seat, tears welling up in his eyes. Roberts must have wanted an earthquake to swallow him whole. "RIGHT. KEMP AND BARNES HAVE TAKEN THE PUNISHMENT FOR THE WHOLE CLASS."

'No one else had the courage to say it wasn't fair. The bell went and Roberts escaped to the staff room and his future. Kemp and Barnes were heroes. Their courage was the talk of the quadrangles, the playgrounds.'

Mr Reid had finished his true story. The class looked at him, glazed by a travel in time to Reid's childhood, lost in self-examination of their own courage, piecing together the meaning of justice. The bell went, but no one was in a hurry to escape.

Pete had forgotten about Lid for the ten-minute story. She now reappeared in his mind. He could see the back of her head; her long, wavy, brown hair. Most boys left the room, Lee went to sort out the goalposts for a quick kick-around.

Lid got up, elegantly Pete thought, from her place. Pete stood. She walked alone to the door. Pete walked to the door about four seconds behind her. He looked beyond into the corridor. Left . . . right . . . there she is. He saw her blue cardigan walking away between reds, blacks, cases, talls, shorts, a corridor filled with the movement of children free for ten minutes. Pete followed. More American cop ideas popped into his thoughts. A chase, an ambush, a confrontation.

He felt a surge of courage. He hurried his steps. He felt his tongue drying up, his stomach knotting. He felt alone without friends to feed from. He closed the gap on the wavy hair and the blue woollen cardigan. Down two steps. He was within an arm's length. He would tap her on the shoulder. Now.

She moved sharply left, pushing open a swing door. He blindly turned the same corner and touched her shoulder.

'Lid, I . . .'

She turned. Her face was not inquiring. It was wide-eyed in surprised disapproval. Her expression halted Pete's words. Something wrong. He looked beyond Lid to a small girl pulling a skirt down over white knickers. He saw a row of white sinks and heard a loo flush.

It took half a second but this was far longer than he was welcome. He heard a shriek, felt his face turn hot crimson, turned on his heels and pulled open the door without a glance over his shoulder at Lydia who was smiling.

CHAPTER 7

Pete's mind was racing. Every time his thoughts slowed down and staggered worn-out to the finish line they found renewed energy and insisted on another lap. He lay in bed and couldn't sleep. His mind was accelerating in full formula-one throttle again. His speeding, confusing thoughts meant he stared at the *Beano* without looking at it, listened to his music without hearing it and lay flat on a crumbly, crumpled, unmade sheet without feeling it.

'Pete,' Mum called from the next bedroom, 'turn it off.' She was grumbling, whining. 'It's half-eleven, now turn it off.'

He swore under his breath.

'And turn your light off too.'

'And good night to you too,' thought Pete. He wasn't angry with Mum. He was angry with himself. He lay back in the hot bed, eyes wide open, and did another few laps.

'You great idiot, why did you rush it; why couldn't it have waited. You could have sat out on the pavement after school, she'd have come and sat down. Now she'll avoid me, think I'm really stupid, the little girl will tell all the year sevens and eights, it was so uncool – couldn't even tell Lee.'

His thoughts cursed, rehearsed and burst. They jumbled, fumbled and mumbled. In the stillness and darkness his bed became more and more uncomfortable. It felt hot, sticky and gritty as if the bottom sheet were spread thickly with warm peanut butter . . .

'He threw off the duvet and stepped softly to the top of the stairs. 'A glass of milk,' he thought, 'some late-night snooker with the sound low.'

He went downstairs in search of peace.

The stairs were very dark. A street lamp shining through the heavy curtains in Mum's room lit the top landing with meagre dredges of light which reluctantly crawled out from under her door. They just gave shape to the darkness and by them Pete realised there were objects on the stairs.

csethicsethicsethicsethicsethicseth
icsethicseth   'thicsethicset
hics   We   'thicsethicse
         cannot   'thicsethi
        discuss   :sethicseth
h.   right and   :sethicset
th   :sethicse
cse.   wrong   :sethi
icse   nicseth
hicse   until   nicset
thicse   nicse
csethic. everyone   ni
icsethic.   eth
hicsethic.   has   et
thicsethic   e
csethicseth enough
icsethicseth   •   •
hicsethicseth food • ...icset
                    ..sethicsethicse
thicsethicsethicsethicsethicsethi
csethicsethicsethicsethicsethicseth

He began to tread down but felt his foot crush something crusty and soft. The light switch was above his head but Mum would be angry. He tried the other foot. It met something

68

Agenda for the Church Council

1   New hymn books

2   Boiler maintenance

3   Church fete

4   Restoration of gargoyles

5   Lawn mower theft

6   Car parking

7   Sponsored walk for the Church Hall damp.

Dying child:

'I'm hungry.'

Jesus: 'I'm starving.'

hard and smooth. He reached down to pick it up. Keeping his balance in the dark he held up a bottle-shaped thing. From an inch before his eyes he read 'Red wine'. What's Mum been up to? he wondered. The bottle was empty.

He held it and tried the next step. He kicked something. A clink of glass hitting glass, empty bottle meeting empty bottle. Being empty, the bottles chonked more than chinked.

He froze. His feet and hands began to feel cold. He couldn't move downwards. The stairs seemed littered with empty bottles. He turned, deciding to go back to bed and find out about the bottles tomorrow. He stepped up and again felt a crusty resistance to his foot. He picked it up, shivering at the thought of a tarantula. It was obvious. It was bread. A loaf of bread with a crushed middle where he'd trodden on it.

Mum's had supper on the stairs, he thought. Yet although he could hardly see, he had the impression that the stairs were stacked with bottles and crusty loaves. He moved upward in the silence.

His foot came down upon a bottle lying on its side. It rolled. Pete lost his balance. His pyjama-clad body fell prostrate, feet-first downstairs. THUMPCHONKCHINKCRASH-WHAMP. The clatter – smashing – banging of bottles, bread, stairs and body filled the stairway, landings and the whole house. The darkness was drenched in pandemonium.

Before the noise had disappeared Pete realised he was lying in puddles of liquid and a light was switched on. He saw that the liquid was red, and as his fingers touched it, expecting thin watery wine, they felt instead a sticky thickness. It smelled of blood.

'Justice,' a voice said.

A small young beggar-looking boy came beside where Pete lay. His clothes were torn and shabby. His hair a mess, his feet bare. But Pete noticed the beggar boy's eyes. They were strong, smiling eyes; mature, twinkling eyes. They were eyes belonging to an old man, experienced, content, wise eyes.

The boy had a begging bowl but his eyes asked for no pity. He stooped beside Pete and dipped his bowl into the sticky liquid. He stood up. Pete noticed that his hands and legs were grimy. He seemed to be working. Having filled his bowl he walked quickly away.

Pete looked for the landing carpet at the foot of the stairs but saw only sand, stones and rocks. He was resting against something firm but jagged.

Another beggar approached. This one was a woman. She was very old and wrinkled. She too was filthy. Grime covered the soles of her bare feet, her arms, her face. She wore tattered garments which hung loosely. She stooped to fill a bowl from the puddles and was joined in the task by another beggar-looking man. Then another. Pete was lying in the middle of several people. Each of them didn't notice him. They all dipped bowls or cups or mugs and having done so walked away.

Then a brown hand reached down from the crowd of beggars and it helped Pete to his feet. It was another woman. Pete turned to thank her but her beauty made him gasp. She seemed to shine at him. Her skin was deeply brown, almost black, and it glowed with red evening sunlight. Her eyes were the wise and deep eyes of the beggar boy.

As Pete looked at her she seemed more human than any-

body he'd ever met. She was full, complete, perfectly herself. Beside her he felt like a polythene bag. He did not understand how he knew that this lovely person loved him. He simply knew he was safe. He felt confident. She said, 'Turn around'.

'Yes,' Pete replied obediently.

He turned and saw the object he had been resting against. It was a splintery wooden post. It stood behind more beggars dipping bowls into the puddles. One of the beggars was the boy, returned to refill his bowl.

Pete raised his eyes and saw the ugliest thing he'd ever seen. His stomach churned inside his body.

The wooden post was a cross. A dead man was nailed to it. The man's ribs were trying to break through thin, tightly stretched skin. His head was flopped sideways onto his shoulder. At his hands and feet the flesh was ripped open, inflamed and bloody. Long metal nails had been driven through them into the wood. Pete felt the pain of the victim. Blood was matted and caked on the man's head, face and dark beard. He was the most appalling mess. Something like barbed wire was in his dark hair. Words were written behind his head. Pete could only see the word, 'Jew'.

The sight was physically ugly but the fact of it was repulsive. Pete thought, 'This man is nothing more than a slab of meat at the butcher's, hanging up on a hook. He is so poor. He is such a waste.' Pete read some violence in comics, even quite enjoyed it, but seeing this made him feel sick. Who could do this to someone? The cruelty, the madness? The man just hung there, abandoned, looking as powerless as dust, more dead than death. Pete had never seen nor experienced anything like this. Here, things were not as they usually were.

Pete's world turned around. 'Who is this man?' he wondered.

'Come, let me show you,' said the beautiful woman. Pete turned to her. Her beauty when he looked at her again, was not only on the outside, on her skin and features. It was also on the inside. It glowed from her eyes in which he saw a tiny reflection of the dead man on the cross.

'Hold my hand,' she said.

'All these beggar people,' Pete inquired, hoping the word beggar wasn't offensive. 'What are they up to?'

'They are evangelists, they carry the message of the cross to others. You can't offend me, don't worry.'

The sticky liquid was blood, and as Pete looked again he realised it was oozing from the wounds of the Jew and collecting in puddles on the ground.

'Who is that man?' Pete asked.

'Come, see,' replied the woman.

Pete was taken where he saw chains on the feet of black people. Each slave was being beaten by whips held by white people. As he looked he saw a mark of blood appear on the foreheads of the slaves and the slaves sang spiritual songs. Their low throaty song filled the scene with hope. There appeared marks of blood on the foreheads of the white people. Chains were being unlocked, wounds were being bound with fresh clean dressings.

The white people said, 'Sorry, we couldn't see, we didn't know.'

The slaves replied, 'We forgive.'

Pete was taken where he saw a multitude of poor people starving. Mothers, with large brown fear-filled eyes, held crying babies to their flat breasts. A man carried his dead child and sobbed beyond consolation. Lines of exhausted, naked children, little more than pot-bellied skeletons, watched Pete

Read Ephesians 2:11-22.

Jesus breaks down barriers †////⟋

There is neither Jew nor Greek, slave nor free, male nor female.

All one in Christ Jesus.

(Galatians 3:28)

Notice how faith in Jesus breaks down racial barriers.
It is as if we become members of a new nation; God's kingdom.
We become citizens of where? (Philippians 3:20)

Jesus broke down the dividing wall of hostility between the Jews and the Gentiles according to the section of Ephesians above. He thus brings peace to racial divides. See verses 14 and 17.
How does the parable of the Good Samaritan declare the same message? (Luke 10:25-37)

Have you any experience of racism? What was it? Should a Christian be racist?

Romeo and Juliet : Across the Barricades : West Side Story : Roots : The Colour Purple : I Know Why the Caged Bird Sings : To Sir, With Love . . .

RACISM HURTS

Heard of Steve Biko?
.... Why not?
Heard of Marcus Garvey?
.... Why not?
Heard of Martin Luther King?
.... Why not?
Heard of Nelson Mandela?
.... Why not?

WHO WRITES THE HISTORY BOOKS ANYWAY?

with longing. They sat beside small, newly dug graves. As each one ran out of breath it tumbled into its grave and the others kicked dirt over its body.

As Pete looked he saw marks of blood appear on the fore-heads of the poor, the starving and the dying. They sang, with foreign tongues, their own songs.

A jumbo jet landed. As its doors opened, loaves of bread cascaded out followed by executive men and women dressed in smart clothes. They were carrying briefcases. Thousands of them walked towards the poor people. A mark of blood appeared on the foreheads of the executives. They began singing in the same foreign tongue.

'What does the song mean?' asked Pete.

'They are singing . . . No more debts, no more interest . . . we return all that is yours . . . your lands, your wealth . . . we return your spirit. Sorry we couldn't see, we couldn't hear, we were sick, please forgive us.'

Pete recognised the song of the poor people for it repeated over and over and over, 'We forgive, brothers and sisters, we forgive.'

All the poor were singing with mouths filled with bread. Mothers' breasts had rich, good milk. The children ran with clothes on their bodies and with bread in their hands kicking dirt into empty graves.

A mark of blood appeared on the graves of the dead chil-dren. The graves opened and the children stood up alive again. They ran to their friends, who gave them food.

Pete was taken where he saw a great and beautiful cathe-dral. It was architecturally majestic. 'Now, this is magnificent,' Pete said. Everything was gold and silver. Frescoes dominated walls and ceilings, fabrics were the finest silks and velvets. It

was a mile wide and a mile high with domes, spires and steeples. The entrance was a huge marble stairway leading to ivory doors inlaid with onyx, rubies, sapphires.

Lower ranks of clergy in the pews were behind higher ranks of clergy. They were clad in ornate vestments. The whole congregation were dressed either like vicars or like bishops and they all stood on different levels. The floor of the cathedral was like a giant's staircase with steps hundreds of yards long. The lowest step was at the back of the cathedral and as one looked toward the front so each step rose upwards. The highest step was at the front and held a high altar table a thousand yards wide. Each step had thousands of clergy all facing towards the high altar. At the back were the lowest, at the front were the highest.

Pete looked and saw blood and a ball of fire burning on the altar table. In a terrible instant the fire grew uncontrollably. An inferno raged before his eyes. In a moment of white heat the whole cathedral was consumed and destroyed.

The fire disappeared and revealed a barren wasteland of ashes and ruin.

A child stood in the far distance. Another beside it. Another stood and joined hands. Soon a long line of children stood and all joined together where the cathedral wall had been. Pete saw the line increasing.

The woman said, 'They are black, white, red, yellow, brown. The children are from every nation.'

Soon the children had formed a human circle ten miles around.

Pete looked and he saw more children climbing onto the shoulders of the circle. There they stood, hands joined together. As a second course of bricks is built upon the first

Hunger

When half the world goes to bed hungry, why isn't it always first on the news?

A poor man is hungry after eating . . .

Portuguese proverb

Thousands and thousands and thousands die every year through the effects of poverty. It has been said that a child dies every 2-3 seconds because of malnutrition and related disease. What makes our consciences dull to world poverty? Read these verses:
Proverbs 14:31 and 19:17;
Isaiah 58 about true fasting;
Isaiah 61:1 and compare it with Luke 4:18;
Ezekiel 22:29.

Jesus and the great prophets were concerned with poverty and the unjust sharing of wealth. Any great prophets reading this?

One-quarter of the world has three-quarters of the world's wealth. Is that fair or what?

The rich part of the world and its banks lend money to the poorer parts of the world. They charge an annual fee to the borrower called 'interest'. When the interest rates shoot up, the poor countries can't afford to pay. They end up paying more back in interest payments than the original loan. The poor countries end up in huge unpayable debt to the rich countries. They starve and have to close schools and cut back on health care just to pay back some of the interest. Contact Christian Aid or CAFOD or the World Development Movement to find the facts. Since 1980, the poorer parts of the world have paid back 1.3 trillion dollars worth of its debt. Has their debt increased, stayed the same or decreased?

DEBT? *Forget it!*

course in a wall, so the rows of children grew higher. All were perfectly balanced. This human building was beyond any circus act of acrobats.

The circle was still ten miles around but now there were three levels of children hand to hand, foot to shoulder. Then adults began climbing, rising up from the ashes. As numerous as ants they climbed the child construction and stood on the shoulders of the highest children.

'From every nation, all colours,' the woman said.

Higher and higher grew the building of human bricks. There seemed no ceiling to reach.

Pete noticed some of the people climbing down. As they reached the ground they walked towards the centre of the circle. There were girls and boys, men and women, old and young. These were those dressed as beggars. They joined hands in a circle perhaps one mile wide. They looked at each other for one second then all turned to face outwards and linked their hands again.

As they turned, the entire building turned as every individual, every human brick, turned to face outwards. The turning was a magnificent kaleidoscope of colours more beautiful, more breathtaking in design, than the cathedral now consumed.

Pete looked and saw that he was standing alone on a vast plain. The sky was black. The air was thundery. Little forks of lightning were acting out a storm far above in the dense clouds. The ground and the rocks stood in sharp luminous bright contrast to the sky. Everything felt expectant. Even the stones seemed tense with anticipation.

But he could only see the horizon stretching away under grey folding skies behind and to the left and right. For before him, standing perpendicular as high as he could see, was a

CHILDREN AND JESUS

He called a little child and had him stand among them. And he said:'I tell you the truth, unless you change and become like little children, you will never enter the kingdom of heaven. Therefore, whoever humbles himself like this child is the greatest in the kingdom of heaven.' (Matthew 18:2-4)

But if anyone causes one of these little ones who believe in me to sin, it would be better for him to have a large millstone hung around his neck and to be drowned in the depths of the sea. (Matthew 18:6)

Read Mark 10:13-16.

What do these verses say about the place of children in God's kingdom?
What qualities have children got that adults need to relearn?
The kingdom of God is childlike . . . Peter, Susan, Lucy and Edmund are Kings and Queens in Narnia . . .

'Today our Church Service has . . .

Adult hymns

Adult liturgy

Adult choir

Adult sermon

Adult words

Adult readers.'

Whoever welcomes a little child like this in my name welcomes me.

'Listen,' Mr Wonka said, 'I'm an old man. I'm much older than you think. I can't go on for ever. I've got no children of my own, no family at all. So who is going to run the factory when I get too old to do it myself? Someone's got to keep it going — if only for the sake of the Oompa-Loompas. Mind you, there are thousands of clever men who would give anything for the chance to come in and take over from me, but I don't want that sort of person. I don't want a grown-up person at all. A grown-up won't listen to me; he won't learn. He will try to do things his own way and not mine. So I have to have a child. I want a good, sensible, loving child, one to whom I can tell all my most precious sweet-making secrets while I am still alive.'
(Roald Dahl, 'Charlie and the Chocolate Factory')

Inner
circles?
NO!

Cliques?
NO!

When the service ends, the worship begins.

'Religion draws its strength from excluding.'

Are we closer to God inside a church or outside?

colossal wall of dark-green diamond-hard ice. It was massive, stretching far to east and west. Like at the end of the world or the universe, the perfectly smooth wall, immeasurably wide and high, was a cosmic-sized dead end.

It was oppressive. Pete shrank in fear before this unnatural glassy wall. He found it hard to think clearly as he was dwarfed to insignificance by the wall. Its perpendicular and its smooth vertical seemed to mock him and the surrounding rocks and uneven ground. Its perfect geometry insulted the rugged natural plain. Its power was humiliating.

He peered cautiously into its menacing surface. Having first thought it was probably mountain-deep and thick, Pete was surprised to realise that while it was dark and dense, there was clearly another side to it. It didn't go on for ever. It was a gigantic divide. It had cut the world in two like a guillotine blade a mile high. Through the dark, opaque ice Pete could see light moving. Clearly the light had superhuman power to have penetrated through this impregnable mass.

Pete heard the woman's voice. It carried her beauty even though she couldn't be seen.

'You can see the light and the life. It gives life to everything,' her voice was worshipping. 'It creates. It is love, the source of all that is.'

'What is this great . . . this big . . .' Pete had no words for the great dividing wall.

'It is the end, it is death, it is all your fear. It is all evil, it is all injustice.'

A question popped into Pete's mind about how he could get to the light but the oppressive power of the wall made the question seem stupid. Clearly there was no way to the light. Yet he wanted to see the light. It was appealing.

'You have only to want to . . . that is enough,' the beautiful voice knew his thoughts. 'Watch, you will see light shine in the darkness. You will see God touch humanity. You will be remade.'

'Can I break through the wall?' Pete asked.

'No,' the voice was final, 'but he does it for you, like Kemp and Barnes did it for you. They suffered that you would go free. So he suffered.'

'Who suffered?'

'The one on the cross.'

Pete thought of the inhuman ugliness of the violent cross and asked, 'Who caused him to suffer? An angry teacher?'

'Love caused him to suffer. NOW BEHOLD,' the voice was raised in loud adoration, 'HE REMOVES IT! THE LAMB OF GOD WHO TAKES AWAY THE SIN OF THE WORLD!'

The voice disappeared. The plain was dark. It was bristling with anticipation. Like a calm before a storm but a thousand times more, as if life itself were about to be born, as if latent natural energies were about to be released. All creation waited. From high up on the vertical glass wall rivulets of blood began to run down. Where they ran the ice was melting so that blood and water were flowing down the sides of the glass wall. It was happening quickly so that Pete found himself ankle-deep in the water.

A wind began to blow and Pete struggled to remain upright in the strong gusts and rising water. Now where the blood flowed down and into the wall flames were licking at the wet ice, sizzling and evaporating the wall. The waters rose to Pete's neck. There was so much steam that he could no longer see the expanse of wall, only the light like a sunrise through fog.

He had to swim now. The wind was violent and the plain had become a rough sea. It was mercilessly throwing Pete from wave crest to trough. He became helpless against the currents and the swell. Thinking he was drowning he fought to keep afloat but was being swamped. He was dumped beneath the surface and no sooner had he risen and gulped the steamy air than he was submerged again. A whirlpool effect was being swept up by the wind.

Pete was being dragged around in a large, wide circle of foamy white bubbling water. He felt himself tumble under and over. The violence of the water now made struggle point-less. Water was forced into his throat, his lungs, his stomach. All was water. Breathing was water. Thinking was water. Water, water everywhere, tossed, turned, around, about, sink-ing, belching, gulping. He was a goldfish under Niagara Falls.

He gave in to the churning, speeding whirlpool. Faster and faster. Spinning and dizzy it dragged Pete, unfeeling, to its centre. He surfaced for an instant just at the moment of being sucked into the very centre where he would be gone for ever. The surface of the whirlpool once white was now blood red. A hand suddenly took Pete's hand and they were finally dragged under together.

'Applause . . . Pete jerks awake.

A colour television. A chin resting over a sliding cue. Two eyes looking carefully along its whole length. A gentle stab at a white ball which rolls perfectly straight towards the black ball. Kiss on the angle. The black ball rolls slowly between the green cushions and drops into the pocket. The white ball touches the cushion and comes to rest, alone on the green baize table. Applause.

Pete looks around. Mum's empty easy chair. A small table beside it. Crumbs of cheese and bread lie on a side plate. A wine bottle with an inch of red liquid in the bottom stands beside it. An empty glass, murky with fingerprints, is poised on the chair's arm.

Pete holds the bottle to his lips and swigs the sharp fruity liquid. He eats a leftover crust and runs upstairs silently barefoot back to bed.

Jesus is a name which comes from the name Joshua, a Hebrew name meaning 'Jehovah is Salvation'.

The word became flesh and made his dwelling among us. (John 1:14)

God or Jesus is described here as the Word. He became a human being and came to live on the earth he had made.

The film director Alfred Hitchcock often cast himself into his films for a brief moment.

Football managers may sometimes come on to the pitch to play.

John explains Jesus' visit to the world like this:
God so loved the world that he gave his one and only Son, that whoever believes in him shall not perish but have eternal life. For God did not send his Son into the world to condemn the world, but to save the world through him. Whoever believes in him is not condemned, but whoever does not believe stands condemned already because he has not believed in the name of God's one and only Son.
    (John 3:16-17)

**God could not sit idly by;
love came to earth to cry and die;
it is for love that we should live;
that's why he died praying, 'Father, forgive'.**

Jesus Don't Go

He comes reeking of beer.
I am gripped by disgust and fear.
He pushes my nightie up. The rest you know,
Jesus don't go.

'Your daddy loved me once.
We kissed and cuddled and enjoyed a dance.'
This month I'll see him two weekends in a row.
Jesus don't go.

They call me names on the bus.
Push my books around, laugh in my face.
I'm afraid, losing weight, can't eat, so
Jesus don't go.

No one taught me to laugh.
I don't love me.
Inside I'm so lonely and low.
Jesus don't go.

Teenager

Job? No.
Figure like hers? No.
Safe at school? No.
Safe at home? No.
Hope? No.
Anyone understand? No.

'I do.'
Jesus.

Come to me all you who are weary and burdened, and I will give you rest.

(Matthew 11:28)

What does the crucifixion of Jesus 2,000 years ago mean for us today?

What happened there, apart from a sad and cruel death?

The answers are given by the first Christians, all over the New Testament.

Try and complete the words . . . The Bible verses will give the clue . . .

Romans 5:10

2 Corinthians 5:19   Rec_____

Mark 10:45   R_____

Ephesians 2:13   B_____ N ____

Ephesians 1:7   Red_____ For_____

Romans 5:9   Jus _____

Romans 3:25

Hebrews 2:17   Ato _____

These words mean little to us today. The writers used jargon of the law courts and the slave galleys and the slaughter house to get across the meaning of Jesus' death.

So . . . what do they mean?

Reconcile
To make up. To make friends again. (Remember how Adam and Eve fell out with God.)

Justified
Just-as-if-I'd . . . never left God.

Ransom
A price paid to release a hostage. (Jesus paid a high price . . . such love.)

Atonement
At-one-ment . . . friends again.

Redeem
To buy back. To purchase the freedom of a person or thing. Jesus bought us back at the expense of his life.

Like all humanity we live far away from life as it should be lived.

Jesus has paid the price we cannot afford, to bring us home to God.

RIGHT. A play in one scene

''old on a sec. Me and God aren't together, right?'
'Right.'
'So me and everything else; wars, rape, pollution, greed,
hunger, oppression, exploitation, all that stuff starts to
'appen. Right?'
'Right.'
'So I die. Right?'
'Right.'
'So Jesus comes and sorts it out. Some'ow 'e 'as to die
to free us from dying and all the other rubbish. Right?'
'Right.'
'So, if I trust this Jesus bloke, then I'm friends with God
again. Right?'
'Right.'
''cause 'e died for me, right?'
'Right.'
'Cool.'

A Life For A Life   by Patricia St John
This is an old story about two brothers who lived in Spain, many years ago, when law-courts were not so careful as they are now.

Luis and Sebastian were twins, and their home was a flat-roofed white house outside the walls of a little mountain town. Their parents had died, but had left them a small in-heritance, and the boys lived on in their old home. They were so alike that no one in the town could tell them apart.

But as the years passed the boys developed differently. Sebastian held a good job; he was kind, steady and hard-working, and everyone spoke well of him. But Luis was lazy and would not work. He cared for nothing but pleasure, and spent every evening gambling and drinking, often not coming home till early morning. In vain Sebastian begged him to leave his bad companions and make a fresh start. Luis just laughed.

It was late one night, and the full moon shone on the white walls of the town. Sebastian sat at the window, strangely uneasy, his eyes fixed on the white ribbon of road that led to the city gates. Luis, as usual had not come in, but somehow tonight his brother could not sleep.

He spotted the running figure even before he heard the beat of his feet, and he went to the door. Luis was running alone, and pushed past him into the house. By the light of the lamp his face showed deathly white, and his clothes were torn and bloodstained. He trembled so that he could hardly speak.

'Oh, Sebastian,' he panted, 'hide me! Hide me! They are coming to take me, and it will be death for me.'

'What do you mean?' asked Sebastian, running to the window. Sure enough, a crowd of people were surging from the town gates, running . . . towards the house.

'We drank too much . . .' cried Luis. 'We fought . . . I didn't mean to . . . he fell back and died. Oh, Sebastian, hide me! What shall I do?'

But Sebastian already knew what to do and was tearing off his tunic. There was not a moment to spare.

'Put on these clothes and give me yours,' he commanded. 'Quick! Stop trembling. Now run out of the back door, and up into the hills, and don't come back for a long time . . . run, brother, run!'

Truly, they were only just in time. Already the noise of shouting and running feet was at their gate. A moment later, the town guard, followed by an excited crowd, burst into the house and drew up short in front of Sebastian. He stood very still, breathing fast, his hair disordered, dirt on his hands and face, wearing the torn bloodstained tunic. They handcuffed him, but he offered no resistance. He walked quietly back to the town jail. A few days later he was tried and condemned to death for murder.

Nearly all the men of the town crowded into that courtroom to gaze at the prisoner. When the trial was over and the spectators sat in the wine houses discussing the case, they all said the same thing:

'How quiet he stood! He did not plead for his life, nor did he seem afraid. "You saw for yourselves the bloodstains on my tunic," he said. "I have no defence."'

'And what of that fine brother of his?' asked others. 'Why was he not at the trial? Nor was he at work this morning. Is he ashamed of his brother, that he lets him die alone?'

But no one knew the answer to that one, and a few days later, Sebastian was executed. A life for a life.

Luis hid in the mountain villages for many weeks. He changed his town clothes for a peasant's outfit and worked for a farmer all through the harvest season. At first he never dared leave his lodging; night after night he lay awake trembling, dreaming of those terrible running feet. But as time went on he grew bolder. He bitterly regretted killing his comrade and longed to see his brother again. 'Perhaps they have ceased to hunt for me now,' he thought. 'Next market day I will go down, disguised, to the town and try to speak to my brother.'

He had grown a beard and stained his face, and no one could have recognised him. Dressed in peasant clothing he joined a crowd of muleteers and went to market. While the bargaining was at its height, he joined a group of bystanders, and started chatting. Gradually he drew the conversation round to the recent murder case.

'I hear the wretched fellow got away,' he said. 'Are they still searching for him, or have they given up?'

'Given up?' replied his companion, turning to him in amazement. 'Our militia never give up! They caught him the same day, tried him in the same week, and he died two days later. There's justice for you! Strange thing is though, there was a brother who disappeared the same day, and has never turned up since . . . some say . . .'

But no one ever heard what some were saying, for Luis gave a strange desolate cry and ran from the market place. Half-blinded with tears, he somehow managed to reach the Governor's house and almost forced an entrance. When the Governor appeared to see what the commotion was about, Luis fell at his feet.

'You have killed an innocent man,' he cried, over and over again. 'It was I, not my brother. Now take me too, for what have I got to live for now?'

The Governor withdrew. After much discussion he returned.

'The law says a life for a life,' he announced. 'If your brother was innocent how could we know – his tunic was covered in blood, and he refused to plead. The case is closed. Go, and keep your mouth shut, and see that you make no more trouble.'

But as Luis turned blindly away, the Governor spoke again.

'Stay,' he said suddenly. 'You are the only brother of the executed man?'

'Yes, yes, there is no one else.'

'Then I have a letter for you. The prisoner wrote it hastily and left it in my care just before he died. I will fetch it for you.'

Seated in the old home, where he and his brother had passed so many pleasant evenings together in childhood and early boyhood, Luis wept and wept. It was nearly sunset before he opened the letter. 'This morning I shall die, of my own free will, in your bloodstained tunic. Now I beseech you to live in my clean tunic. I send you my love and God bless you Sebastian.'

And Luis understood. The waster, who had lived for himself and fought and murdered, must be counted as dead in the prison. The man who had loved and suffered and sacrificed must go on living. It should be so. He sat thinking till the early light glimmered in the room. Then he rose and flung off his dirty disguise. He washed and dressed himself in clean clothing, as Sebastian would have done, and went out to meet the new day.

It was the third hour when they crucified him. The written notice of the charge against him read: THE KING OF THE JEWS.

'Eloi, eloi, lama sabachthani?'
Mark 15

I know men and I tell you that Jesus Christ is no mere man. Between him and every other person in the world there is no possible term of comparison. Alexander, Caesar, Charlemagne, and I have founded empires. But on what did we rest the creations of our genius? Upon force. Jesus Christ founded his empire upon love; and at this hour, millions of men would die for him.

Napoleon Bonaparte

There in the garden of tears,
my heavy load he chose to bear.
His heart with sorrow was torn.
G. Kendrick

Compare Luke 22:39-45 with Mark 14:32-42 with Matthew 26:36-46.

This is an account of real anguish.

What decision did Jesus have to make?

Where did he get his courage from?

CHAPTER 8

Pete knew he needed Mum's permission to go to the disco. All his plans with Lee and with Lydia depended on Mum's 'Yes'.

But they were his plans. 'Why must I ask Mum,' he thought. 'It's my life. Who does she think she is?' Yet he wanted to ask her. He wanted to feel that she was in charge, that she knew where he was. At times Pete wanted to be away from home. At times he wanted to be just a little boy curled up on Mum's lap. It was his Ready Brek feeling; young enough to enjoy it, too old to admit it.

He would tell Mum he was going to the dance. It would be his way of asking.

He was in bed reading comics. He was probably well enough to go to school but felt a bit churned up in his stomach, as if he'd drunk several glasses of cold water straight down. His head ached too. These slight symptoms were a good excuse to build upon his main reason for avoiding school.

The day after an embarrassing show-up is unbearable in its taunts and humiliations. Even teachers in touch with the playground scene can be just too clever. He could hear Floyd (French), 'Don't put your hand up if you need a slash, just put my glasses on.' Or Renshaw (Humanities) would nudge him matily and whisper sarcastically from the corner of his mouth, 'I've got some magazines you can borrow, wink wink.'

Lee would probably go for 'Phantom Flasher' as a nickname. But it wouldn't last. Two days afterwards, the heat begins to cool and the colour begins to fade. By then the victim is armed up with the passing of time.

'Living in history are we?' or 'Doesn't anything new ever

happen in your life? Must be boring.' Pete would practise these responses before school tomorrow.

Mum came into his room with the vacuum cleaner switched on. The flex was at full stretch back to the socket in her room. Soon she would have to switch it off to replug it into the socket in Pete's room. She was busy. An excellent chance to ask, to tell, her. She didn't look in the mood for a sit-down chat. He fixed his eyes on the comic but watched Mum for signs of her blue slipper moving to the 'Off' switch.

The motor died. She had pulled the plug out of its socket by stretching the flex too far.

'Damn,' she left the room and returned seconds later with the three-pin plug in her hand.

She knelt beside Pete's bed and grappled with the plug behind his sound system.

'Mum?'

'Yeah?' She made contact and the vacuum burst noisily into life again.

'Mum?' But she couldn't hear now.

'Mum?' Pete yelled. She stood up, looked at him and kicked off the motor.

'What is it?' Her voice carried the impatience of unnecessary nursing.

'I'm going to the club disco on Friday.'

'Oh you are ill, aren't you!' she didn't disguise the sarcasm. 'Who are you going with?'

'Lee, who do you think?' He pretended to be affronted by her maternal interest.

'Oh no one, just thought you might have a fancy woman . . . Lydia, for instance?' It was her playful tone now. Ruining Pete's attempt at independence she smiled, and he blushed

involuntarily. He covered his face with his comic and held back his laughter.

The vacuum motor started once more.

'How the heck did she know?' Pete wondered. 'Why does Mum know what's inside me?'

He lifted his comic. Her back was turned. He spoke aloud, 'Yeah, Lydia, she loves me. We're going to the disco, then we're going to run away together.' He thought about describing his sexual ambitions but didn't trust the noise of the vacuum cleaner that much.

Just before four o'clock in the afternoon Pete got dressed. He enjoyed not having to wash and brush his teeth. It was a fun break from schoolday routine. He put on Saturday clothes.

Mum was watching TV. Pete walked past her and slipped out of the back door. He felt braver after the day in bed. The change in routine had softened his embarrassment.

He crossed the council green and sat on a stone water hydrant. The sky was deeply blue and any wispy clouds were very high. The afternoon was quiet. The housing and roads were sleeping until school ended. It was still and warm. He felt fine.

Two girls walked into view from between the end of a terraced house and a cheap brown fence. It was Lydia . . . good. And it was Karen Alsop . . . bad.

How do I get this girl on her own without snooping into the lav again? he wondered.

They strolled aimlessly towards him. They weren't in a great hurry to arrive home and begin the several hours of homework.

Pete felt too conspicuous. He wondered about hiding and then stepping out, as if by coincidence, as they walked by.

Karen could be heard first. 'Has the geography got to be in tomorrow?'

'Yes, second lesson,' Lydia replied. 'You going on the field trip?'

'Yeah.'

'Same here.'

'See you, then . . . oh, can I ring you up if I'm stuck on the maths?'

'OK.'

'Byeeee . . . be good.' Karen giggled and then kept on walking. Pete knew they had started the homework chat just before they came within his hearing.

'You're not dying, then,' Lydia turned to Pete and came towards him.

'Naw.' Then there was a long pause.

'I haven't told anyone,' Lydia said. Hope rose in Pete's stomach.

'Not even Lee?' If Lee didn't know, the future looked possible.

'No.'

'Honest?' Pete was smiling with relief. The whole incident which Pete imagined being announced to a school assembly ('. . . was found snooping, prowling around the female lavatories . . .') was shrinking to nothing. A sleepless night, a day in bed, all for nothing. He could have hugged her.

'What did you want?' she asked, leaning her head slightly sideways.

Pete tightened again, his relief now strangled.

'Why did you follow me?' she asked. Pete wasn't sure

Homework excuse

'Sir, I couldn't do my homework. The dog ate it.'

'Send it for an X-ray and hand it in on Monday.

Follow with a poopa-scoopa and hand it in on Tuesday.

Make Rover sick and hand it in on Wednesday.

I'll call round with endoscopy and look

at it on Thursday.

There's never any excuses so

HAND IT IN ON FRIDAY.'

Why do schools set homework?
(Put a tick against the answer you think is right.)

1   It helps you practise the day's lessons.

2   Schools like messing up your free time.

3   It helps you get a job.

4   Parents want it.

5   It makes the school look good.

6   It is healthy.

7   Schools don't know why they set homework.

8   It is good for you.

9   It is bad for you.

whether she was being friendly or cross. Words like 'Nothing' or 'There was no reason' or 'It don't matter' all tried to force their way between his shut lips. But it had been too great a mistake to have no reason.

'Well, I was nervous.' He tried honesty but it was difficult.

Sundays

Long lie in, easy easy duvet warm.
House silent after Saturday night.
HOMEWORK BECKONS . . .
Longer lie in, duvet warm.
Better ring Tom. Better ring Kath.
Breakfast forgotten. Smell veg peeling.
TEN-THIRTY KICK OFF . . .
Long lie in, snuggle down, duvet warm.
CAR BOOT SALE . . .
Like a bargain, perhaps a bargain.
Save money, save money, money, money, money.
SHOPPING . . .
Like spending money, like spending money.
Yeah, I'll do the geography this evening after
THE MATCH
THE SALE
THE SHOPPING . . .
Like spending money, easy easy warm like duvet.
'Why don't I go to church on Sundays?
I never give it a thought.'
HOMEWORK . . .

'Nervous about what?' she asked. If only she would stop asking and let me think, he said to himself. He twiddled grass in his fingers and couldn't look at her eyes.

'What were you nervous about? She was trying to help him find words but was stifling him by the interrogation.

'It's this weekend,' he began.

'What is?'

'Pete looked up and saw a bicycle approaching. It was clearly Lee.

'The parachuting,' he lied. He looked her between the eyes and feeling that even a man could be afraid of parachuting said, 'I'm afraid of heights and don't want to jump.'

'You wouldn't jump, silly, that takes months of practice. Did you expect to freefall twenty thousand feet on your first visit?' She walked away to her garden gate.

Pete was just feeling that this small mockery was better than the big one, as Lee drew alongside. He had seen them talking.

'Wotcha,' Lee was grinning all over his face, 'well . . . is she coming with you?'

'Yeah . . . no sweat,' Pete grinned and made a circle with his thumb and first finger, 'putty in my hands, son . . . Putty in my hands.'

The second lie to Lee was easier than the first to Lydia.

Pete was very good at bravado, but he hadn't got the hang of humility yet.

The club room wasn't large enough for all the young people who filled it. It was difficult for the leaders to count exact numbers, because the only light was multicoloured flashes

keeping time with the loud beat. The atmosphere was heavily crowded and dark. Pulsating blue, red, green, white lights. A flash would reveal heads and faces moving in random motion. A bubbling burst of white light made the room into instant X-ray. This disappeared and the green light showed everyone framed half a second later than the X-ray. The strobe flickered and turned the room into a glinting cartoon of frozen snap-shots.

'Hea . . . vy rap; romping and a-moving and a-stomping to the tune.

'Get . . . that . . . rat; 'bout time you learned how to fight how to rhyme and show them you ain't be the stereotype they want you to be . . . that's a fact . . . that's a fat fact.'

The bass speaker buzzed and pounded the air. It was hot. It was sweat hot. The music was very loud.

Pete and Lee were yelling to each other in one corner. 'WHERE IS SHE, THEN?' Lee was demanding into Pete's left ear.

'I DUNNO, DO I?'

Pete had kept the pretence of a success with Lydia going all week at school. It had been fun. Lee was close enough to Pete eventually to recognise Pete's failed attempt to ask Lydia. Pete was close enough to Lee to allow him to share the failure. Like mountain climbers enjoying the safety of each other and base camp after an abortive attempt upon the sum-mit, the boys shared their adolescent weaknesses and their strengths. But Pete had kept the story alive, perhaps for his ego, and both enjoyed the fantasy. They often enjoyed an unreal vision of something in the future; a motorcycle tour of Europe next summer; converting an attic into an observatory to house Lee's telescope. The unreal was manageable. The real, like Lydia, was not.

Rumour, or wishful thinking, stated that she would be at the disco. But they had waited now for one hour, drinking ginger beer from plastic tumblers. She hadn't turned up, They didn't dance, or even tap their feet. They never did. Already they were making plans to leave, to buy some chips and cider and drop in to Lee's to watch the evening film. His dad would be there but he was OK. He just sat drinking too much sweet sherry and saying little.

'LET'S SPLIT,' Lee yelled into Pete's ear. Pete nodded in return and they moved towards the narrow door through the tight crowd of bodies.

A white flash. Something exploded powerfully near the DJ. A scream. The music failed. The lights failed. Darkness. Another scream, then another. Pete and Lee stopped and turned with their backs to the door. More panic screaming.

'Fire!' someone yelled from the DJ end. It was probably a joke but the crowd were afraid of the crush and the dark and the explosion. The crowd, as one, ran towards the narrow door, pushing, shoving, stamping, grabbing, pulling, shouting.

Pete and Lee, off-balance, facing the wrong way, collapsed like matchsticks to the ground, watching each other, faces grimaced, through stampeding legs, socks, boots, shoes and bare feet which pummelled and pummelled their heads and bodies. Others fell on top of them. The weight was crushing the air from their lungs.

'I can't bear this any longer,' Pete thought in distress. Then he lost consciousness.

Pete was looking over the shoulder of an old man who was writing. His scribing sounded scratchy. His words and letters were unfamiliar to Pete; a foreign language.

Were they in a cave, or a stone-walled room? Pete wasn't sure. The floor had a matted covering. The room was slowly brightening as if dawn had crept in unnoticed and had begun unpacking. The writer's candle had burned low and was probably not needed now.

The man continued to write but was aware of Pete's silent presence behind.

'Welcome fellow-traveller,' the man spoke so gently and cheerfully. Pete recognised a warmth and beauty in the voice. It sounded familiar.

'Welcome, you have come far.' It was a greeting for an expected guest.

'Forgive my not getting up but I must write it down. It must be written. It is more important than you. It is more important than me. It is more important than life.'

Pete saw a wooden three-legged stool in front of the man's writing table and went to sit on it. He watched the writer working, scratching long unbroken rows of shapes the size of capital letters. The room grew brighter and faint warm shafts of morning sunlight came slanting across the room. The candle continued to flicker. The man continued to write.

'Even death didn't finish him,' the gentle scribe murmured to Pete as he scribbled.

'Even death, life's dead end, didn't finish him,' he blew out a tiny laugh from between his aged lips.

'He's made a new life now, a life for us beyond death,' his voice rose with his mirth.

'And it's here now too. It's here now. I must write it down. Tell the world.' The man blurted out the simple sentences as if part of a marvellous tale unfolding, which he urgently wanted to share.

'Did you see him crucified? Dreadful. Would finish the best of us off. Not him. Alive again. Hallelujah!' He gleefully shouted the last word, startling Pete.

'Are you just making all this up? Are you just writing a story for someone?' Pete thought the man might be an eccentric storyteller, a doddery old fool.

The man beamed such a smile at Pete that his face seemed like the rays of sunlight. His old face lit the room, shining together with the sunbeams.

'O my dear friend. Beloved fellow-traveller.' The man stopped writing and sat back. As he began to answer Pete's question, Pete felt his inside burn with a fire of new life.

'How could we make it up? Some of us have already died for speaking out. If we had been lying, like you do, would we have let them stone us to death?'

Pete felt the wooden chair hard beneath him and fidgeted uncomfortably.

'The women saw him first, you see. Look, I've just written about the women. I've got to write it as it is. If I were making it up I'd leave out the women. They'll think we're mad putting in the women. But they did, so I must. He loved women.'

The old man's enthusiasm was catching even though Pete could not understand his reasoning.

'My dear fellow-traveller, don't you believe me? Why don't you believe me? We have seen him alive again. We have touched him, we have eaten with him.' He spoke kindly, softly, lovingly.

'Did he die on the cross? Perhaps he didn't. Perhaps you only thought he'd been dead.' As Pete spoke he even wondered himself where his scepticism came from. It pushed up from beneath his growing excitement.

'Dear, dear friend,' his kind, wise eyes spoke of love and of suffering. Pete could not take his eyes away from the appealing light of the old man's eyes.

'We loved him. We knew him. We saw him die.' The candle on the table guttered and went out, leaving a trail of smoke rising. 'Did we see a sickly man rise from his tomb? O my friend, we saw a new man, a Prince, a Lord of Life, a man filled with heaven on earth. We saw a Resurrrection man, the first. And now he fills us, my son, he fills us.'

Pete burned with a yearning for what he could see in the man's eyes. The old man continued to write, smiling, murmuring, 'Yes, yes,' occasionally, as if remembering. The little room became filled with the fresh glory of a golden sunrise.

The writers of the accounts about Jesus are called evangelists.

Why did John write his account? John 20:31.
Why did Luke write his account? Luke 1:1-4.
What does 'gospel' mean?

Do you think the differences between the four gospels make them more, or less, realistic? Why?

RESURRECTION

Jesus did not stay dead according to the evangelists. He came back to life the same but different. It was as if he had entered a new dimension beyond the usual limits of a human being. This is called his resurrection. It was a rising to a new life.

Some good reasons for believing in Jesus' life beyond death . . .

1 *Jesus said he would:* Matthew 12:40, 27:63, Mark 8:31, John 2:19-22.
We count Jesus as the best teacher the world has known. We still study his words in school. Why dismiss what he said about his rising?

But did he really say these things???? If Jesus is all just a made-up story, why aren't there thousands and thousands of stories about people as astonishing as Jesus? Surely if people made it all up once, other people could have made up other such accounts about God-like people down the centuries. But the accounts of and the person of Jesus are unique.

2 *There were many eye-witnesses who saw Jesus alive after the crucifixion* Read the end of all four gospels. Read about Saul in Acts 9 and read 1 Corinthians 15:3-8.

3 *People died for speaking out about Jesus and his rising* They could have changed their story. Do people give their lvies for what they know isn't true?

4 *The Church began because of it and still celebrates it on Easter Sunday* A crucifixion without a resurrection is not a reason for a celebration. After seeing Jesus die the first followers had nothing to celebrate. It looked like it had all finished.

5 *Women are put in as eyewitnesses* This is totally at odds with the culture of Jesus' day. If it was invented it is extremely unlikely that a writer would have used a female eyewitness. Women couldn't give evidence in a Jewish court all those years ago. A Jewish prayer includes: Thank God I was not born a woman.

'It was a man's world!'
'It still is!' (Woman)

6 *His tomb was empty* The opponents of the first
Christians threatened, flogged and killed them for
their faith. But they could not disprove it. Jesus'
dead body would have silenced the new faith. But it
was not there. 'The silence of Christ's enemies is
as eloquent a proof of the resurrection as the
apostles' witness'. (John Stott)

**7 *Frightened followers of Jesus changed into
fearless men and women soon after Jesus'
death*** Something very very powerful changed their
grief and fear into missionary courage. 'The
disciples were not gullible, but rather cautious,
sceptical and "slow of heart to believe". They were
not susceptible to hallucinations. Nor would strange
visions have satisfied them. Their faith was
grounded upon the hard facts of verifiable
experience.' (John Stott)

**Christ rises from the dead,
and by his rising he
delivers us from anxiety
and terror: the victory of
the cross is confirmed,
love is openly shown to be
stronger than hatred, and
life to be stronger than
death.**

Kallistos Ware

I know of no one fact in the
history of mankind which is
proved by better evidence
of every sort to the understanding of a fair enquirer,
than the great sign which
God has given us that
Christ died and rose again
from the dead.

T. Arnold

Pete sat on the ambulance bench opposite Lee. 'I'm not here. This is happening to someone else,' Pete thought and wished. 'Lee and I have caught the bus. We've paid our fares. We are sitting on the bus.'

Pipes. Oxygen mask. Red chunky packs of blood and plasma. Lee on his back, bare-chested.

Reality slapped Pete hard across the face.

'Here we are. I'm sitting in an ambulance. Lee is lying in an ambulance, half-alive, half . . .' He couldn't think the word. Not Lee. Not real flesh-and-blood Lee. In fact Lee seemed only flesh and blood now. A body, bruised and broken and messy.

Pete looked outside. The glare of a blue light, pulsing like at the disco, ran alongside the speeding, swaying vehicle as if desperately trying to keep up. Traffic lights swept past. McDonald's came and went, W. H. Smith, Boots, Saxone, Lloyds' green black horse, blue Barclays,TSB,Link,fruitand-veg.gap,Rackhams,Rackhams,Rackhams,Rackhams, Ratners, Millets,save pounds,save,save,save.

'They'll all be shopping tomorrow,' Pete thought. 'They won't know about Lee or me.' The shops seemed so dull to him. He didn't even think of compact discs as Dixons fled by. He wanted Lee more.

'Live, Lee. You'd better live,' he willed.

The laboratory of life-saving equipment sped on like a guided missile.

Later, the back doors were opened. A scrum of nurses and porters appeared framed by the back of the ambulance. Trolleys clanged, steps opened. Pete watched his friend

wheeled out from under his eyes. Everyone hurried. Pete thought for a split second of a student rag week and a bed being pushed for money-raising, but reality was too close to daydream. It sat heavily like a vulture on his shoulder.

A nurse seriously asked Pete if he was able to walk and seriously asked him to follow her. Pete seriously followed.

'You his brother?'

'Yeah . . . no, I'm his friend.'

'What happened?'

Pete couldn't think. He shrugged and said with more adult expression than he was used to, 'I'm sorry, but I feel awful.'

'That's OK, matey, sit here and I'll get you a drink.' She was kind.

The hot chocolate in the plastic beaker was from a vending machine. Pete sat, lonely and insecure. He was keenly aware of his surroundings and situation; something very frightening at the disco, an ambulance ride; Lee unconscious; a man working hard pumping Lee's chest; hot chocolate; a pay phone; empty bench seats; a receptionist. It was all prodding him to act very grown up. A tear was on his lips before he knew he was crying. He couldn't control the sobs. They came from his spirit and insisted. 'Is this grown-up?' he wondered.

A nurse came to the receptionist and spoke quietly. Pete was close enough and still enough inside himself to hear their whispers.

'The young boy they just brought in must have died at the accident. Is that his friend over there?' The nurse nodded towards Pete and met his nervous red eyes.

She began walking towards Pete.

'Dead,' Pete's mind said. The room felt cold. The white walls were mist and snow. 'Lee,' it said. The nurse's brown

shoes came nearer. 'Spit Nolan dead and gone for ever,' it said. 'Tell me about the rabbits, George,' it said. His mind heard a shot. He saw a Snow Goose circling above a beach being strafed with machine-gun fire. He saw barbed wire and bodies in a sea smoking with war. Love called to love. A kestrel in a dustbin with its neck wrung. Dead and gone for ever, it said.

Pete stood and was surprised to be as tall as the nurse.

'Do you have your friend's telephone number?' she asked. Her eyes were friendly, like a vet's putting dumb animals to sleep.

'Lee was a friend of mine,' Pete said.

The plastic cup hit the floor and spots of hot chocolate splashed the nurse's tights.

CHAPTER 10

At any moment Lee will walk through the back door, Pete thought. He was sitting quietly with his mum in the kitchen. They were both red-eyed and yet-to-get-dressed. She was browsing over a Sunday magazine and Pete was leaning on his hand looking absent-mindedly through the window. A cyclist was coming along the road. Pete stood up. Mum looked up. It was a paper-boy on his way back to the newsagent's. Pete sat down.

'I'm sorry,' Mum said gently. She had said it many times since last night.

Pete's stomach was knotted in fear. 'What am I afraid of?' he wondered. He felt waves of anger too. Anger at Lydia, anger at Mum. Already his pursuit of Lydia meant nothing. It was drowned by strong feelings of not forgiving her for not coming to the disco.

If only we'd been dancing or looking the other way. If only we'd left earlier. If only I hadn't pretended she was coming. Pete's thoughts were giving him a headache. How would he ever stop the flow of 'if onlys'?

He had slept badly. He had woken early and a few seconds' peace had been crushed by the booming memory of last night. It had felt so heavy that he could hardly lift his body out of bed. When his mind wasn't numbed by disbelief it was attacked by 'if onlys' which persevered like trained soldiers.

'What we gonna do, Mum?'

'How do you mean?'

'Well, can't we do something?'

'Like what, love?' she asked gently, with understanding, but her eyes were wells of tears again.

'Should I go to Lee's house?'

'I shouldn't, love. The police will be there, and they'll come here.'

The fear tightened again in Pete's inside.

'Oh well,' Mum sighed, 'I'll peel some spuds for lunch, life must go on.'

'How can life just go on?' he wondered. 'Just go on as if nothing has changed. Lee's dead. Where's he gone? He was alive. He'd said, "Let's split". He was so alive. How can you just die? Not even a road accident? How did he die? Why didn't I die? Lee, why didn't you stay alive?' he spoke the last question out loud and Mum turned from peeling the potatoes. She just smiled knowingly and warmly. Pete was angry with Mum, but he did feel very close to her at this moment.

'Mum, how can you be alive one minute and dead the next?' It felt like a silly kind of question, but asking it seemed to help.

Mum shook her head slowly, 'Life can change course so quickly, Pete.'

'But it was only a disco,' he said angrily.

'I know, Pete, I know. I'm sorry.'

He went upstairs, slotted a CD in and threw himself face down on his bed. The numbness robbed him of more tears.

All Sunday the clouds hung low. It drizzled after lunch and during the evening. No wind or sun came to disperse the lethargic weather. Pete too felt only lethargy. He nibbled at lunch unhungrily. He sat staring at the TV, only occasionally concentrating on the programme. He quickly pressed for another channel when an ambulance appeared on the screen and when some teenagers were shown bopping. The minutes and hours dragged by but Pete sat in his timeless bubble of

apathy, feeling more and more nervous, more and more sick.

The police hadn't stayed long. Lee was another statistic. Mum called the doctor who gave Pete something to slow down the memories and 'if onlys' and something to help him sleep.

On Monday Pete looked for Lee in the bike shed, in the chair that stood empty beside his school desk and in all the playground areas. He talked to Lee during maths. But mostly he just sat like he'd sat watching TV; vacant, preoccupied, gone away.

Lydia had asked Pete about it.

'Why didn't you come?' Pete confronted her, finding confidence in his sadness and anger.

'I never go to the club,' she replied truthfully. The futility of Pete's fantasy nudged him back into depression. They'd waited at the disco, knowing she would never come.

On Tuesday Pete stayed in bed. On Wednesday he went, with Mum, to the funeral.

Pete sat with his mum on a hard wooden church pew at the back. There was no one else on their pew. People were scattered around the other pews mostly in pairs or threes. Towards the front of the church there were more people grouped together. A woman Pete didn't recognise had her right arm around the shoulders of another lady. Her wracking sobs were audible above soft organ music. The atmosphere was sober and solemn. People wore very straight faces. Any smiles would have been as quickly chased away as a farmer shoots at rabbits.

Pete wasn't crying. He sat on his hands and looked around.

He felt numb inside as if his body had showed up but left his emotions behind. His mind was a house left empty by a family away on holiday.

He counted the people. Thirty-seven . . . no, thirty-eight. The soft music, which had gently stroked the ears and hearts of the thirty-eight, faded quietly away. A silence took its place, broken only by sobs from the front like the irregular pulse of someone fatally wounded. Pete's mum reached into her bag for a pink paper tissue and blew her dripping nose. Pete tapped a foot but the echo was embarrassing and Mum touched his arm to say, no.

The main church door opened just behind them. A tall clergyman walked through holding an opened book. He wore the same pure white nightie Pete had seen on TV. Underneath the nightie was a long black skirt which came to the man's ankles. As he walked slowly forward Pete noticed an inch of denim jeans underneath the skirt. The man suddenly announced slowly in a clear, loud voice,

'Jesus said, I am the resurrection, and I am the life; whoever believes in me, though he die, yet shall he live, and whoever lives and believes in me shall never die.'

Something caught Pete's attention. He began to think hard. What was it? he thought. Like with a feeling of *déjà vu*, Pete struggled to remember what it was.

The vicar was followed by four men in heavy black coats carrying a coffin on their shoulders. The light-coloured wooden coffin was recognisably smaller than others Pete had seen. He was disturbed thinking of Lee in the coffin, and was surprised by a rush of warm, close feelings towards his friend. He would have liked to say something out loud, but under his breath instead said, 'Goodbye, mate.'

Lee's mum and dad walked in behind the pallbearers. His dad had shaved and greased back his hair. The point of his white shirt collar folded slightly upwards.

As soon as the clergyman had settled everyone into their places, he stood beside the coffin and started to speak. Pete heard some words of welcome and a page number given, like a teacher reminding a class where they've got up to in their reading book. But although he found the pages and stood when the others did, he didn't sing or say the prayers or listen to the vicar.

He mostly felt uncomfortable there. It was a best-behaviour place. He watched the vicar, the backs of other mourners, the still coffin and his mum's pink tissue becoming more screwed-up and soggy in her fist. He searched his mind again to catch the fleeting experience he'd had at the start.

The vicar said, '. . . suffering and death on the cross', and Pete saw a picture behind his eyes of a cruel and brutal ancient execution of a thin, deathly man with barbed wire in his hair. He knew that he had seen it somewhere before. It was ugly but it reminded him too of something very whole and beautiful.

Pete noticed Mum's sobs and saw her hand reaching for his own. She grasped it and Pete remembered the drowning, choking water, the white whirlpool become red, the hand that had held his own at the last.

The vicar read, 'The last enemy to be destroyed is death.' The dreams flowed into Pete's consciousness. He saw from the cliff height the beauty of the sky and the sea. He felt the perversions under the water. He remembered a wading through chocolate and the surge of love that gave him courage to leap from the basket.

And light filled his thoughts. Light from eyes and voices. He wanted to have this light for himself. And at the same time he remembered the love. The woman had loved him, the old man had loved him, and Pete realised that the one on the cross loved him and the whole world. He wanted that love for himself. And he thought of being very much alive. He felt an urge for life. 'He is alive, he fills us,' the old man had said. Pete wanted this sense of life, he wanted to be full of it. He looked at the coffin. Then he squeezed his mother's hand to reassure her.

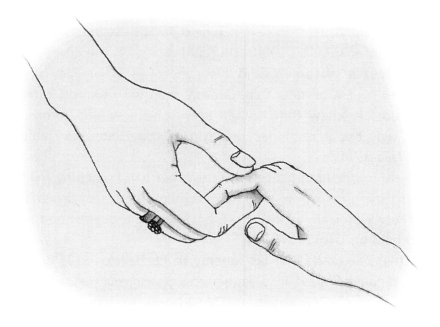

Amazing
Remarkable
Incredible
Unbelievable
Good News
Fantastic
Brilliant
Mega
Astonishing
Wonderful
Excellent

Romans 6:4
'. . . just as Christ was raised from the dead through the glory of the Father, we too may live a new life.'

'What, even me?'

'Yep.'

'Stop getting so excited; you're embarrassing me.'
'But it is pretty amazing, you have to agree.'

Therefore, if anyone is in Christ, he is a new creation, the old has gone, the new has come!

2 Corinthians 5:17

When you're dead you're dead.
<u>Wrong</u>. Jesus has made
that statement untrue for
those who trust him.

Death be not proud, though some have called thee Mighty and dreadful, for thou art not so.

John Donne, AD 1609

Where, O death, is your sting?
Paul, *c* AD 55

I asked a friend nearing his death from cancer how his faith was. He replied, 'My Lord has kept me these last 65 years. I have no reason to doubt him now.'

Steve speaking to Gerald, AD 1994

A Prayer For You . . .
Pray it every day until it comes true.
Then pray it every day.

Lord,

I'm sorry and determined to leave wrong things alone now and always.

I want to be filled with your Spirit now and always.

I want your new life now and always.

I want to know you, now and always.

128